D1241309

The Long Way Around

By Jimmie Hand

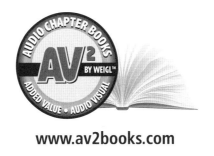

www.av2books.com

Your AV² Media Enhanced book gives you a
online audio book, and a self-assessment
activity. Log on to www.av2books.com and
enter the unique book code from this page
to access these special features.

Go to **www.av2books.com**,
and enter this book's
unique code.

BOOK CODE

E732941

AV² by Weigl brings you med
enhanced books that support
active learning.

AV² Audio Chapter Book Navigation

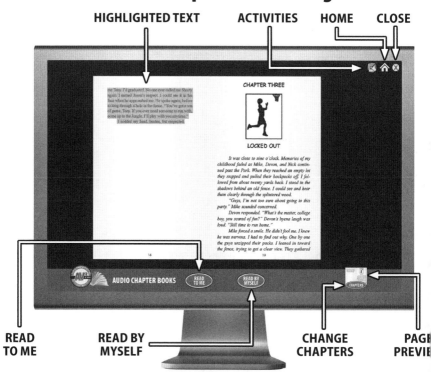

HIGHLIGHTED TEXT   ACTIVITIES   HOME   CLOSE

AUDIO CHAPTER BOOKS   READ TO ME   READ BY MYSELF   CHAPTERS

READ
TO ME   READ BY
MYSELF   CHANGE
CHAPTERS   PAGE
PREVIE

Published by AV² by Weigl
350 5th Avenue, 59th Floor
New York, NY 10118

Website: www.av2books.com www.weigl.com

Copyright ©2014 AV² by Weigl
All rights reserved. No part of this publication may be reproduced, stored in
a retrieval system, or transmitted in any form or by any means, electronic,
mechanical, photocopying, recording, or otherwise, without the prior written
permission of the publisher.

First Published by Scobre Educational Press.

Library of Congress Control Number: 2013937469
ISBN 978-1-62127-994-5 (hardcover)
ISBN 978-1-62127-950-1 (single-user eBook)
ISBN 978-1-48960-025-7 (multi-user eBook)

Printed in the United States of America in North Mankato, Minnesota
1 2 3 4 5 6 7 8 9 0 17 16 15 14 13

062013
WEP310513

2

TABLE OF CONTENTS

CHAPTER ONE

LOCKED UP

"Step inside." A prison guard grabbed my arm and pushed me through the heavy doors.

This can't be real, I thought. *This can't actually be happening.* I stared straight ahead.

I held my hands in front of me and the guard unlocked the cuffs. My wrists were swollen. They hadn't hurt this badly since the state championships.

I marched down the center of the prison. Angry voices bounced off the concrete walls. The noise came from the men behind the bars, my neighbors. I held back my tears and did as I was told, following the guard. We walked up a staircase to my cell.

"Stop here," he yelled. So I did. I was always a good listener. Every teacher and coach I'd had could tell you that. I learned how to listen from my Mom. She made a point of only saying things once. I don't remember much about Dad. He left when I was six.

Mom said he wasn't real nice to us. We never heard from him again.

I stepped into my tiny cell. The door slammed shut behind me. I turned toward the back wall. Two beds leaned against opposite walls. The place was barely lit, but I could see that someone was in one of them. He was rolled up in a blanket sound asleep. I stared at him curiously. Then I looked above me and noticed that the ceiling was falling apart. Water dripped to form a puddle in the corner. I stepped away from the stranger's bed. I noticed a dirty toilet and a sink towards the back. There were no doors, no privacy. A light with a metal screen over it flashed and buzzed above my head.

Slowly and quietly I made my way over to a bed. I sat down with a loud creak. A deep sigh came rushing out of my mouth. I was facing seven years inside this room, four years if I got out on parole. *How was I ever gonna do this?* I wondered. I leaned back and closed my eyes.

In an instant, I was back on the football field. That was the place where everything was perfect for me. I was throwing a pass to the sideline. My best friend Billy was wide open. The sun was shining and the defense was in slow motion. I heaved a pass down the field and watched the ball spin through the air.

My cellmate let out a snore. The sunshine disappeared. The smell of freshly cut grass was gone. All I could smell now was the metal box I was caged in. I peeked over at him. He had salt and pepper hair. His thick moustache matched a shaggy gray beard. When he rolled over on his bunk I saw that his eyes were open. I looked away quickly, my heart racing in my chest. The man didn't say a word. Instead, he snorted a few times. Then he was back to sleep as if I wasn't even there.

I leaned back on my thin cotton mattress. The metal wire beneath me cut into my hip. I was taken to the New Mexico State Prison on a big black bus at dawn. That was six hours ago. It was a horrible ride, I was all chained up. And I was scared—as scared as I've ever been.

The ultimate humiliation came when I was issued my prison uniform. There was a number printed across my bright orange shirt. I was no longer Matt Devon, senior in high school. I was no longer a kid who loved football, his mom, rap music and cars. I was K763921. I was a number. I was used to wearing a number on my football jersey, number fifteen. This felt very different.

I laid there on the bunk trying to get my mind off of my surroundings. I closed my eyes and tried to sleep. I tried to focus my thoughts on life before jail. Right away I thought of Amy. Amy Rogers had been my girlfriend since we were eight. We grew up together. We did everything together. The two of us had big plans. She was going to be a lawyer and I was going to play in the NFL. Tears started to roll down my checks. Our plans were over now.

I couldn't ask her to wait seven years for me. I knew it would be better for her if we broke it off. I'd already caused her enough pain. She had sat by my side through all of this.

Last night they told me I would move to the state prison at dawn. And I knew what I had to do. I looked Amy straight in the eyes and asked her not to come see me anymore. I asked her not to think about me. I told her to forget she ever knew me. That was the hardest thing I have ever had to do.

I was born and raised in Hobbs, New Mexico. Hobbs is a small town in the southeast corner of the state. We're right near the Texas border. We lived on the outskirts of town, but not on a farm or anything. I lived with my mother and my seven-year-old nephew, Kenny. My older sister, Katy, ran away awhile back. We only heard from her once, a year later. She dropped by to leave a baby boy on our doorstep. Kenny was just two months old when he came to live with us. I was ten at the time. Kenny always seemed more like a little brother than a nephew.

When Mom died a year ago, Kenny and I were all that was left of our family. I had just turned seventeen. That was when everything began to fall apart.

All I ever dreamed about from the time I was five was playing football. Baseball and basketball were okay, but only to keep me busy until football season. I was born to throw the pigskin. People always told me that my right arm was special.

Most of the youth football teams developed their game plans around the run. But with Billy as a receiver and me throwing the ball, we mainly passed. Billy Bryant was my best friend in school. We were always working on our game together. I can still picture him running slants, outs and buttonhooks in my backyard. We'd practice until the sun went down. He was the fastest kid in school and had the best hands. We played together all the way through high school. We never lost a game together. Not even when we played those big Texas high schools.

A loud bell rang that jolted me back to where I was. My cellmate sat up, throwing off his blanket. He rubbed his face with his right hand. Our eyes met and he looked at me for a long time. "Chow time," he finally spoke in a gruff voice. "Is this your first time in the joint?" he asked.

"Yes sir," I replied.

He gave me a strange look. "They told me I was getting a new roommate. So you were some hotshot high school quarterback, huh? I read about you in the paper."

"I was a quarterback, but I'm no hotshot, sir."

He looked at me strangely again and shook his head. "Mind your own business while you're here. The less you say the better off you'll be. You're a big guy, you should be okay." He was right. At six-foot-three and over two hundred pounds, I was pretty big.

But that didn't mean I wasn't scared.

My first dinner in prison went okay. In the movies, bad things always happened in the cafeteria. Luckily, nobody tried to take my food or mess with me. I did see two guys arguing. Although they nearly came to blows, a guard was on the scene quickly.

After moving through the food line I went to a table and sat down. I didn't speak a word to the strangers around me. The food was gross. I could barely swallow a bite of it. I left thirty minutes later, relieved that I'd made it through my first meal.

When I got back to my cell I felt safe. Then my cellmate sat down on his bunk and looked at me for the longest time. "So I read about you, but I'm not sure I believe what I read."

"Which part, sir?" I said trying to speak in a strong voice.

"Stop calling me sir, will ya?" He reached back and scratched his neck. "My name's Al Pancano. Call me Al."

"Yes, si-" I stopped, "Al, I mean." I reached my hand out to shake with his. " Matt Devon."

Al sat back down after shaking my hand. He shook his head with a smile on his face, "Why would a kid like you rob a liquor store?"

I didn't know how to answer him. "It's complicated," I said. "It's a long story."

He leaned back on his bed, "Well, you've come to the right place to tell long stories."

CHAPTER TWO

MY BIG MISTAKE

They say that every man in prison has a sad story. I was no different. So with Al leaning back in his bed, I told him mine.

High school is supposed to be the best time of your life. For me, this was only half true. On one hand, I was the captain of the football team. I had a girl-friend and was a good student. By my senior year every major football program in the country was re-cruiting me. On the other hand, life was hard. During my junior year Mom suffered a heart attack and passed away. I was seventeen. My life flipped upside down.

Up until that tragedy, things had been pretty easy for me. We never had much, but Mom always put food on the table. When Mom died, everything changed in a hurry. We were broke.

After Mom's funeral, I did a lot of thinking. I sat down with Amy and her parents a week later. I told them I was dropping out of school. There seemed to be no choice in the matter. I had to look after Kenny. And I couldn't do that without money and a job. I made a joke to Amy's father, "I like school, sir, but the pay really stinks." Mr. Rogers laughed. Then he told me how crazy I'd be to give up on school. I had to find a way to make it with Kenny for another year. Then I would graduate. I would sign with a major college football program. They would make sure that I was taken care of—and Kenny too. If I was patient, everything would work out. I listened to his advice closely. He gave me a number I could call for a part-time job.

I began working at his cousin's hardware store the following day. This meant that I had to miss a few practices, but Coach understood. I was very busy. I'd pack Kenny's lunch, drop him off at school, go to school myself, work, and then head to practice. While the memory of Mom's death still haunted me, I was getting by.

The good news was that we were winning football games. The biggest distraction in my life wasn't football. And it wasn't dealing with the death of my mother either. Money was the biggest issue in my life. Kenny needed money to join the Boy Scouts. He needed money for new sneakers and clothes. At the end of each month, we could barely afford groceries.

The only bright spot in my life was the promise of a great future. A number of colleges offered me full scholarships. These scholarships included housing, food, books, and living expenses for both Kenny and me. All I had to do was make it a few more months.

Deciding on where to go to college was fun. Every day Kenny would take out all the pamphlets and catalogs that I had received. We'd explore campuses through pictures of football fields and libraries. Kenny had his mind set on Ohio State. I think it was mostly because of their uniforms. I was considering a number of schools but hadn't made my final choice.

On a rainy Friday afternoon, I attended my last football meeting as a Roosevelt Roughrider. The season was over. We'd just won the state championship for the second straight year. The meeting only lasted about an hour. Coach made a speech. A few players spoke too. Then we all ate pizza while the seniors discussed their future plans. For most of these guys, their football careers were over. They talked about studying history next year or taking over the family business. As for football, Josh Stewart was going to Texas Tech, Billy was heading to Oklahoma, and I was still undecided.

By five o'clock that night, I was on my way home to see Kenny. I assumed that Kenny would be in the living room watching television. But when I came through the front door the house was silent. The television was turned off.

"Kenny?" I called out. My voice echoed up the stairs. I stepped out of the living room and peeked into the kitchen. "Kenny?" I yelled louder. Right away, I heard a muffled groan from upstairs. Something was wrong.

I ran up the stairs and into Kenny's bedroom. He was curled up in a ball on his bed. He was soaked with sweat and grabbing his stomach. "What's wrong, Kenny?"

"My stomach hurts, Matt." Tears streamed down his cheeks. "I'm really hot too."

I rushed over to the bathroom sink and wet a towel with cold water. My hands were shaking as I grabbed a thermometer from the medicine cabinet. Leaning over him, I stuck the thermometer in his mouth. I could tell he was in pain. *I wish Mom was here,* was all I could think in my head.

I was still a kid myself! I'd never even taken my own temperature before. Everything was overwhelming me. *How long did I leave it in there for? How the heck do I read this thing? Should I call the doctor?* I was panicked.

Two minutes later I read the thermometer. Kenny's temperature was 103 degrees. I had to get him to a doctor. I carried him down the stairs, out the door, and into my truck. The ten mile drive to the hospital felt like forty.

Kenny was set up with a bed and a doctor arrived soon after we got there. I sighed, relieved for the moment. I was so scared on that drive over to the hospital. Kenny was the only family I had left.

I sat in the waiting room for about thirty minutes. "Matthew Devon, Mr. Matthew Devon." A nurse's scratchy voice called out to me.

"Yes," I paused, "Is Kenny Devon okay?" I spoke quickly. "Do you know what's wrong with him?"

The nurse handed me a few sheets of paper with questions on it. "You'll have to ask the doctor. Can I see your insurance card please?" She asked politely.

I knew there was going to be a problem. I had to cancel our insurance last year. I spoke softly to the woman, "I don't, I mean, Kenny doesn't have any insurance. You see, my mother passed away about a year ago—"

She cut me off. "Well, how do you plan on paying then?"

This was a good question. I hadn't planned anything. I was whispering now. "My nephew got sick and I didn't know what to do. So I brought him here."

"Well, we can't keep a patient overnight without insurance. Would you like to pay cash?"

"Cash?" I spit out.

"If not—"

I cut her off this time. "Cash is okay." Alarms were going off in my head. *What if they sent him home? What if he got sicker? What if he died?* "How much cash?" I asked, reaching into my pocket. I had thirty-seven dollars in crumpled bills.

"Five hundred dollars for an overnight stay."

"Five hundred dollars?" My heart raced in my chest. "Sure, no problem." I acted like I had the money. "I'll just go get it and then I'll be right back." I left the hospital in a panic. I had no way of getting that money.

I got into my truck and drove down the dusty road back to my house. I knew that Kenny was in the best place right now. The longer I could keep him there, the better off he'd be. *Where am I going to get five hundred dollars?* I wondered.

I didn't realize that the hospital wasn't going to send Kenny home. They would have treated him and sent me the bill in the mail. I didn't know that at the time. After talking to the nurse I was sure that Kenny's life was in my hands.

Sweat started forming in pools beneath my armpits. Everything started to spin around me. I felt like I might pass out. Immediately, I jerked my truck over to the side of the road. I parked it and turned off the engine. I placed my head in my hands and cried. "What should I do, Mom?" I looked up to the sky. "I don't know what to do. Why did you have to leave me, Mom?"

Wiping away my tears I began to think. A light flashed in my head– the bank! But as quickly as this light flashed, it went out. I remembered what Mr. Leon had told me when I applied for a loan last month. "We can't loan you any money until you're eighteen. New Mexico law, Matt." My eighteenth birthday wasn't for another two weeks. So for the next fourteen days, the bank was not an option.

Ten minutes had passed with me sweating in the front seat of my pickup. My plan so far was to take a loan out from the bank in two weeks. That way, I could pay back whoever loaned me the money tonight. The question was: Who was going to loan me the money? I could ask Billy's parents. But Mr. Bryant just lost his job at the factory. They were having trouble making ends meet themselves. They wouldn't be able to help. Next, I thought about Amy's family. But they were in worse financial shape than the Bryants. I went through everybody that I knew in Hobbs. Finally, I came to the conclusion that nobody could help me.

In my mind, this left only one option. A feeling of sadness came over me when I finalized my plan. I knew that what I was about to do was risky. I also knew that it was illegal. But when I closed my eyes all I thought about was another funeral—anything was better than that.

I pulled into my driveway ten minutes later and jumped out of my truck. I raced into the house and up the stairs. My first stop was Mom's room. I hardly ever went in there. I passed through her doorway. I knew that Mom wouldn't be proud of what I was about to do.

I stepped around her bed and walked with purpose into her closet. Then I climbed a short ladder that led to our attic. The attic was filled with worthless junk draped in spider webs. I reached down to lift up a broken-down air conditioner. Beneath it was an old brown shoebox. I remembered hiding in the attic once when I was little. My father told me never to go "snooping around" in the attic. But when he went out bowling one night, I did anyway. After I saw what was inside of that box, I never opened it again. But I always knew it was there.

When I ran out of options the shoebox was what I came up with. I flipped off the lid carefully. Sure enough, it was still there. My eyes widened. I was staring at a pistol. Like many things in that attic, the gun didn't work anymore. It didn't even have bullets. That was just fine by me. I hated guns, and the last thing I wanted to do was shoot someone. I picked it up and stuck it on the inside of my belt. My next stop was Don's Liquor Store. I was going to hold the place up. When I turned eighteen in two weeks, I would take out that loan from the bank. Then I could return the money I was going to steal. The way I pictured it in my head seemed okay. The gun had no bullets in it, so nobody could get hurt. Everything would work out.

Needless to say, my stupid plan didn't work out. I wasn't a criminal and I had no idea what I was doing. I pulled up to the liquor store and my heart was beating through my chest. I walked into the store quickly, moving right up to the register. I pointed my gun at the clerk. "Give me five hundred dollars!" I screamed.

The clerk was an old, hard-looking man. He

looked more angry than scared. He slowly reached beneath the register for a paper bag. "You want five-hundred, you said?" The man spoke calmly. And then, "Pop!" He pulled a gun from beneath the register and shot me in the stomach. I fell to the floor with a thud and he shot me again.

I laid on the floor bleeding. The last thing I remembered before passing out was the sound of sirens.

I ended up back at the hospital. Kenny was having a routine surgery to remove his appendix. I was on the third floor, near death. It would be two weeks before I awoke. A doctor told me that I was lucky to be alive. I sure didn't feel lucky. After being moved to a hospital bed in the county jail, I was officially a criminal.

Two weeks later I was found guilty of attempted armed robbery. I was sentenced to seven years in prison. How quickly it all fell apart. Kenny was placed in a group home. As for me, I'd ruined everything. Every college that was interested in me took back their scholarship offer. In one night I ended my football career. With one bad choice I lost my girlfriend and put my nephew into an orphanage. In one night, I ruined my life.

I hated myself when I walked through the doors of the New Mexico State Prison. My life was hopeless and pointless.

CHAPTER THREE

MAIL CALL

I told Al my story on my first night in prison. He went on to tell me his. Al had also made a bad decision that changed his life. He drove his car while drunk and fell asleep at the wheel. He nearly killed the young girl he hit. He said that he will never be able to forgive himself.

It was pretty weird that we were cellmates. I was a football player and Al was a sports agent—before we were convicts, that is. If things had gone differently for both of us, we may have met anyway.

I always imagined prison being the place where time stopped. Sure, there were definitely days when everything seemed to slow to a crawl. And there were plenty of times when I thought I was losing my mind. Still, before I knew it, I'd been in prison for three years.

There are things that happened that are hard for

me to talk about. I was beat up quite a bit when I first got here. Usually there would be about three or four of them. They'd come at me all at once so there really wasn't anything I could do. Maybe they did it because I was so young. Maybe they did it because I was the new guy. After a while, I quit trying to figure it out. Eventually they got bored and stopped.

I hated prison. It wasn't just the fights. And it wasn't the terrible food either. I hated not being able to see the people I loved. I hadn't seen Amy or heard her voice in over three years. And I refused to read the letters she sent me every week. I felt like I didn't deserve her.

I spent most of my time working in the prison kitchen as a baker. When Mom was alive, one of her favorite things to do was bake. I thought about Mom all the time while I was working in the bakery. Al was the head baker. That made my life a little easier.

Every day, we'd get about an hour of free time in the yard after work. Someone was always throwing a football around. I must admit that I was tempted to join in at times. But I remembered what Al told me my first day here: "Mind your own business." The last thing you wanted in this place was to be noticed.

One day, a football found its way over to my feet. I had my first difficult choice in a while. *Should I throw it back?* I picked up the ball and squeezed it. I hadn't touched a football in three years. I was surprised and excited by the way the leather felt in my hands. Electricity moved through my body. I wanted to fire a bullet back to whoever lost the ball in the first place. Instead, I did the smart thing, tossing the ball back underhand.

I went back inside that afternoon and thought about my life. There wasn't much else to do in jail. No long drives, no restaurants, beaches, vacations or stars. I would think about what I'd done a lot. I couldn't believe how stupid I was. After "lights out," those thoughts would die down. I would just lie on my bunk and think about Amy. I'd even try to remember her voice sometimes.

After touching that football, I knew what my dreams would be like. Sure enough, when I closed my eyes that night, I was on the field. It was right near the end of my senior year and we were pitted against Lubbock Central. They were the number three ranked team in Texas. It was like I was really there. I could hear the music in the background, I could feel the mud in my fingers as I picked the clumps from my cleats.

Billy and I watched films over and over during the week leading up to that game. The cornerback guarding Billy was playing in his first year on varsity. Although he was a good player and a great athlete, he was inexperienced. We'd found a weak link.

I pictured the first series. That was the one where we twisted their cornerback into a pretzel. The pictures in my head were detailed. On first down, Billy ran a 12-yard slant. I threw the ball low where it could only be caught by him. He stiff-armed the cornerback and nearly broke free.

On the next play we did the same thing on the opposite side of the field. This time Billy went a little deeper. Another first down as we marched toward midfield. We tried it again on the next play. This time Billy faked an out and then slanted in. The corner got pretty close to stopping this play. Still, Billy managed a sliding catch.

We now had the defense exactly where we wanted them. In the huddle before the next play I noticed the young cornerback smacking his helmet. This was a signal to any football player to "wake up." We'd successfully gotten into his head. I was sure that if we tried another slant he'd be waiting for it. On the next play Billy lined up facing the inside, again. The cornerback inched closer to the line of scrimmage. He didn't want to be embarrassed by us again. I called hike quickly and Billy cut across the middle. It appeared that another slant was coming. Right as Billy passed the middle of the field, I pumped my arm hard. Sure enough, the young cornerback lunged forward. He thought he had a sure interception. Instead, Billy stopped and turned his slant up the field. I tossed the ball forty yards over his shoulder. He caught it on the eight-yard line. Nobody was near him as he strutted into the end zone for a touchdown.

I woke up smiling the next morning in my damp

prison cell. When I dreamed about football I always woke up happy. Yet, there were countless other nights when I would wake up crying. These were nights when I'd think about Mom, Kenny, and life without Amy. I couldn't get her out of my mind.

Once a week, I would get a sweet smelling letter from her. I would hold it to my nose and start to open it. Then I'd stop, placing it in a box beneath my bed. She never quit writing to me, not in three years. It pained me to receive a letter from her and not open it. But I was sure the pain would be worse if I read her words.

Still, mail was something I looked forward to. Kenny was almost eleven now and his letters always made me happy. Reading about his adventures really gave me a boost. He was a happy kid. He loved school and batted third on his baseball team. He played quarterback in youth football, too. What really made me happy was Kenny's foster family. About two years ago the Hendersons had officially adopted him. I'd never felt so lucky. Every weekend he went down to the stables in Albuquerque and rode on Hank, a brown horse they owned. Kenny even sent me a picture of him riding Hank. I kept it on the wall next to my bed.

I heard from Billy once in a while too. He was up at the University of Oklahoma playing wide receiver. He sent me videotapes all the time. I'd watch them in the library whenever I got the chance. Billy had grown into a star. He visited me around the holidays every year and always sent me letters. He'd end each letter by telling me that I would be joining him soon in the NFL. I smiled at the thought of this, but never really took it seriously.

I'd been lifting weights every day for the past three years. I lifted because I was bored, not because I was going to make a comeback. Either way, by the end of that third year I was like a tank. I'd built up as much muscle as any NFL quarterback. I thought about football all the time. But I knew that taking four to seven years off and trying to play in the NFL was impossible. Billy meant well, but he didn't understand what prison had done to me. I didn't believe in myself anymore.

While looking through my mail one day, I passed a letter from the University of New Mexico A & E. I looked at it strangely before opening it. *Why would a college be writing a letter to me in prison?* Something was a little off. *Wait a minute*, I thought. The handwriting on the letter looked familiar. I quickly pulled one of Amy's letters out from the box beneath my bed. They were identical. "Nice try," I said aloud. And I tossed the letter under my bed with the others.

"You got a letter from a college?" Al asked.

"No, it was from Amy. She figured out that I wasn't reading her letters and–" This thought made me sad. I couldn't finish my sentence. I wondered if Amy missed me the way I missed her.

Al noticed that my eyes had welled up with tears.

"It's time I tell you something, Matt."

There was an expression on his face that I couldn't read. "I had a girl too. Janine, she was the love of my life. When I came here six years ago, I was a mess. When I got locked up, I gave up my life. But Janine was stubborn, like Amy. She wrote me letters all the time." He paused for a long time and finally continued. "And then the letters stopped coming, Matt. Think about that."

With this comment still hanging in the air, Al left the room. It was TV night and the guards left our cells open from eight until ten.

I stared back at the letter. Suddenly, I was panicked. *What if this was the last letter Amy ever sent me?* I reached down and grabbed the letter from the box. I flopped down on my bunk. *Why had she used stationary from New Mexico A&E? Had she found someone else? Was her new boyfriend a professor there?* My curiosity began to run wild. After a few agonizing minutes staring at the letter, I tore it open.

The letter began:

Dear Matt,

I hope that you read this letter. I've been writing you every week for three years without even an "I'm still alive" postcard.

You once told me that we would always be soul mates. You said nothing could come between us. Why did you quit on us?

I want you to know that I still love you and I always will. I will write to you until the day you are released. I'm not releasing you from your promises. You promised me that we would be together and I'm holding you to that.

You're probably wondering about the New Mexico A & E stationary. Well, I've been in contact with the head football coach and told him about your situation. He remembers you. He said he thought you were the best high school quarterback he'd ever seen. He would love to have you come and play for him when you get out.

What do you think? Aren't you the kid they said was born to throw the football?

I'm coming to visit you next Saturday. Our dreams can still come true. If you are waiting for me when I get there, I'll know that you want me back in your life.

I love you,
Amy

Tears streamed down my face as I read her letter. For the first time in years I was hopeful and excited. Amy still loved me. And I still had a chance at my football dreams. Sure, I'd made a mistake. I'd paid the price too. I'd spent some of the best years of my life alone, behind bars. Now it was time to move on. Amy was right. My life wasn't over. I couldn't wait until Saturday.

CHAPTER FOUR

VISITORS

Less than twenty four hours before Amy's visit, I leaned back and closed my eyes. I was a nervous wreck. I tried to visualize my life after prison. For the first time since I landed here, this future life included Amy. Although I didn't know exactly what I would do for a job, I knew there was only one thing I'd ever wanted.

"Hey Al, what do you think a guy's chances are of playing pro ball after sitting out a while?"

Al perked up. "Checkmate," he called out, winning his tenth game in a row. "Depends on the guy. How good was he when he decided to sit out?"

"Pretty good," I spoke modestly.

"I heard he was better than that," Al smiled.

We both knew who we were talking about. "But what if I only played one year of college ball at New Mexico A&E?" I added. "Could I get drafted?"

"You'd have to have a phenomenal year." Al was pretty blunt. If I was going to have any chance of playing in the NFL, I would have to be exceptional in college. It was a long shot. Al wasn't finished. "If that coach gives you the chance, you'll make it happen."

"You really think I could do it?" I started to smile confidently.

"If you want it badly enough. You're going to have to make up for some lost time. You've been in the weight room, so that's good. Still, guys your age already have three years of college experience. It's going to be tough. " Al was right. I had a lot of ground to make up.

After what seemed like an eternity, Saturday arrived. I paced the floor all day until a guard appeared at my door. He opened my cell and I followed him to the visiting room.

The large area resembled a high school cafeteria. The only difference was that it was surrounded by armed guards. My eyes scanned the room in a flash. Amy hadn't arrived yet. I sat down at a table and chewed on my fingernail for a minute. Then, from the corner of my eye, I saw her. Suntanned and smiling in a white, sleeveless dress, she was more beautiful than I remembered.

We walked toward each other. Tears welled up in Amy's eyes and rolled down her cheeks as we hugged. "Hello," was all I could say to her at first. When I finally sat down I breathed a deep sigh. Our eyes were still locked on one another. "You are so beautiful," I finally managed to say.

We talked about everything for the next few hours. About Kenny and how well he was getting along. About her school and how she liked studying law. I didn't want to ruin our moment, but I had to say something. Before she was there ten minutes, I had to get something off my chest. "I'm so sorry for doing this to us. I should have come and talked to you before I robbed that store. I'm sure I wouldn't be here today if I had."

"It's in the past now," she whispered.

"And I should have kept in touch with you. I can't believe I gave up on us. I'm so sorry that I hurt you, Amy."

"It's okay, Matt. I've never been mad at you for not writing me. I just wanted this whole thing to be as easy on you as possible. I've just kept loving you."

I squeezed her hand and changed the subject. "I like your dress, Amy."

"Thanks," she said. "And you look great too. You always looked good in a uniform." We both laughed.

"What's that?" I asked her, pointing to her hands.

Amy had been holding a box since she sat down. She opened it in front of me. Inside was a thick notebook, some videotapes, and a football. "Coach Copeland gave me these to bring to you. He's the coach up at New Mexico A & E."

I couldn't believe the size of the play book. It was fifty times thicker than the one I had in high school. Holding it in my hands was exciting. "Look at the size of this baby!" I said, smiling.

"Coach Copeland told me that they throw the ball about seventy percent of the time. They recruited two wide receivers last year who can really fly too. They'll be juniors when you get there," she said.

"You really got all this done, Amy. This is unbelievable." I proudly held my new stuff under my right arm.

She smiled. "No big deal."

"So what kind of guy is Coach Copeland?" I asked, excitedly.

"Well, you can tell me because you'll get to talk to him tomorrow. He's going to call you," she said.

"Really?" I gripped the football in my hand and felt another rush of excitement run through my body. I wanted to dance. I wanted to celebrate. I wanted to lace up my cleats and play. Still, I knew there was a long road ahead. After all, I hadn't been paroled yet. I stared at the football, deep in thought.

Amy forced a smile. "You look good Matt. You seem happy."

I kissed her. "Now that I've got you back I'll always be happy."

The four hours of visiting ended in what seemed like ten minutes. The buzzer sounded. "No, it can't be time yet, can it?" I asked as I stood to say goodbye.

"It won't be long until I have you all the time," she said softly. And I watched as she walked through the doors and left.

The next day Coach Copeland called. We had a conversation that made me even more excited to get out of jail. Coach Copeland and I got along great. We spoke a common language—football. He said that maybe this whole thing happened for a reason. He told me that, "most paths to greatness don't go in a straight line." He was really going to give me a chance to play.

Eventually, we went over the play book. I had a few questions, but everything was pretty much straight-forward. Just before he hung up, he advised me to get in some practice throwing the ball. "Just throwing for an hour or so every day can make a huge difference by next year." I knew I had to find some decent receivers. The only guy I could think of was Al.

I did find a guy the very next day. Bobby Moore was about 6'1" and 190 pounds. He was as fast as they come. He'd played some wide receiver in high school, but his real love was track. He was nineteen years old. Last year, his senior year of high school, he'd been the state champion in the one-hundred meter sprints. But Bobby started hanging out with the wrong crowd. He ended up driving a getaway car for two of his friends who had just robbed a house. Even though he didn't rob the house himself, the police arrested him anyway. He was sentenced to two years. Bobby said that he would have been an Olympian if he hadn't gotten into that car. Once again I saw what one bad mistake could do to someone's life.

During the next few weeks, Bobby and I would head off to the side of the yard every day. We'd run slants, outs, and deep posts. It seemed strange throwing a football after almost three years off. It was just like riding a bicycle, though. It all came right back to me. After a few weeks of practice, I was throwing harder and more accurately than ever before. I attributed this to the muscle I had built up.

The next year of my life went by very slowly. I played football in the yard and saw Amy as much as I could. My bond with Al grew even stronger. By September I was finally just a few weeks away from my parole hearing. If everything went according to plan and I got paroled, I would be out of prison in about a month. I would have served four years of a seven-year sentence. Just thinking about being in the real world made my head spin. I couldn't wait.

Al was also getting ready to be released. His hearing was just a few months after mine. He assured me that we'd both get paroled. Still, I was nervous about it every single day.

Finally, the hearing arrived. I wanted to sound smart, but not overconfident. I wanted to make sure they knew that I was sorry for what I'd done. When I got into the room they asked me why I felt I deserved to be paroled. I opened my heart to them without a script. I told the truth about my lapse of judgment. We talked about the guilt and shame I felt over the past four years. It was obvious to the parole board that I was sorry. I would never do anything illegal in the future under any circumstances. Their vote was unanimous—I was going home, and just in time for the holidays!

Christmas at home was a dream come true. I was finally a free man and it was more than I could have hoped for. I saw Amy every day and I got to see Kenny too. We tossed the football around in the back-yard together for an hour. I was really impressed by the strength of his arm. Our time together made up for some of our lost time. It was very emotional for both of us. He told me how much he appreciated what I tried to do for him. We decided that it would be best for him to stay with his adopted family. They were great people and Kenny felt comfortable with them. The good news was that they lived only ten miles away from New Mexico A & E. This meant that I would get to see Kenny all the time once college started.

Dinner was a real treat. It was the best food I had eaten in years. Before we ate though, I held up my glass and made a toast "to coming home." Then I got down on one knee and asked Amy to be my wife.

She said yes, of course.

CHAPTER FIVE

NEW MEXICO A & E

Everything was moving along better than I could have hoped for. Kenny was doing well. Amy and I were engaged. Al was about to be released from prison. The future appeared bright. This made me even more anxious for spring practice to roll around. I knew that Coach Copeland would give me a chance. But after spending four years in prison, I was unsure about my abilities.

On a cold day in January, I drove up to the New Mexico A&E campus. I had been let out of prison just two months earlier, so I had just missed the football season. When I made the drive from Hobbs to Taos, I was excited to begin college. I would have a few months of adjusting to do before spring practice started for next season. I stepped out of my car and took a deep breath The air never smelled so sweet. I was a college man. I knew that Mom would have been proud.

I made my way up the stairs and down a long hallway to my room. College was pretty much the way I pictured it. The biggest difference in the picture was me. I walked through the thin corridor leading to my room. A few skinny freshmen stared at me like I was an old man. I realized that things were going to be a little different than I expected. When I opened the door to my room, things got a lot easier.

My roommate looked like a giant. He was curling two of the largest weights I had ever seen. He stood up to shake my hand and offer me a friendly smile. His name was Toby Karvas. He was a 6'8" tight end. Although we played different positions on the field, we were very similar. He was coming in as a freshman after spending four years in the Navy. He was my age, twenty two. Coming in, I was nervous about being the oldest freshman on the team. I was sure that I'd be an outcast. Meeting Toby made things much easier for me.

We talked a lot that night about high school football memories. That was the last time either of us had played. His high school team and mine played each other during my senior year. I reminded Toby that we'd won that game pretty easily.

The first few days of adjusting to my new surroundings were pretty easy. I was having a lot of fun being a college student. When I paid Coach Copeland a visit I quickly realized that my journey had only begun. I walked toward his dimly lit office and knocked on the door a few times before entering. Coach waved me in and seemed excited to see me. "Matt Devon, we finally get the chance to meet." Coach smiled and shook my hand firmly. I returned his smile.

Although I was trying to focus on Coach, I was distracted. The light from the window shone directly onto a green chalkboard. The chalkboard had the names of all the players on the team penned in neatly. We continued to talk, but Coach could see my focus was on the chart. I was surprised to find my name listed as the number four quarterback. Seeing three other names ahead of mine rattled me. But what could I expect? I'd never played one down of college football. I had to prove myself before I climbed to the top.

Coach saw the disappointed look on my face and spoke. "Don't worry about the chart, Matt. That's just where we left off last season. New guys always start at the bottom."

I looked at some of the rest of the positions. I saw that Toby was listed as the fourth tight end. "I understand," I said. "That's only fair."

"Sit down." I did. Coach got serious. "Some of this is going to be an adjustment for you. You've been gone a while. These guys have been playing a heck of a lot of football. Don't get me wrong, I expect you to play well. But take your time and let the game come to you."

Amy had written letters to every school that offered me a scholarship four years ago. None of them responded. Nobody wanted a convict quarterback. Nobody wanted me representing their school. But Coach Copeland believed in second chances. He was willing to offer me one. So when he spoke, I listened.

"Coach, I just want you to know that I'll do whatever it takes. If I have to carry the water jars, I'll do it. I really appreciate the chance you're giving me here."

"You gave yourself this chance, Matt."

We shook hands again and I left. My dreams were still within reach. I would need a great season to have a chance at going pro. But I'd have to win the starting job first. I couldn't show NFL scouts anything from the bench.

The week before the official start of spring practice, the four quarterbacks met. We spent about two hours throwing footballs. We talked about footwork and fundamentals. I was listening, but mostly, I was watching my competition. The other guys knew one another and I could tell they weren't too happy about me being there.

Brent Barber was going to be my stiffest competition. After watching him, I thought that I probably had the stronger arm. In the end, I knew the starting would be his or mine. Brent was also the guy who was the most annoyed by my presence.

I was sore when I awoke the next morning and

grabbed the paper. I hadn't thrown that many passes since high school.

A headline in the sports section distracted me from my soreness: **New Mexico Lands New NFL Team.**

That's right, NFL football was coming to my home state. The New Mexico Grizzlies would play their first game one year from now. I didn't want to get too far ahead of myself. Still, I started to daydream. The Grizzlies would need a quarterback. All of this could work out.

An hour later, I got a phone call from Al. He'd been out of prison for two weeks now. He sounded about as happy as anyone could sound. He was planning on heading up to Taos to watch me play in the "red and yellow game," our annual scrimmage on the last day of spring practice. "Hey kid," he paused, "You all right?"

I could sense he had something important to say.

"Yeah, everything's going great," I said. "I'm the fourth-string quarterback." I laughed.

"That'll change in a hurry," he assured me.

"I hope so. How are things? Is the shop opening soon?" I quizzed.

"Six weeks," he answered. Al had purchased a baseball card shop in Hobbs. This was his lifelong dream.

I was staring at the newspaper when Al asked,

"I guess you've heard about the new team, huh?"

"Yup." I could feel something coming. "Al, what's bothering you?" I asked.

"Nothing. I just know what you're thinking. Those guys will start playing about the same time you finish with A&E, right?"

"Yeah, I gave it a thought." I paused and then continued. "I know, I haven't even played in my first college football game. I'm number four on the depth chart, and I'm thinking about the NFL. I'm getting way ahead of myself." My own self-doubt led me to make this statement.

"No, nothing like that! I think you could jump right in with the Grizzlies tomorrow," Al corrected me.

"Then, what's the problem?" I asked.

"You can't play in the NFL if you're on parole. The league won't let you."

I was shocked. I had never even considered that. I didn't know what to say. "Are you sure?"

"That's the rule, I checked this morning."

"So what do I do?" I asked, trying hard to control my emotions.

"This is not that big of a problem, Matt." Al got hyped up. "You're off parole in two years. So you play one year at A&E and then one year up in Canada. The extra experience will be valuable in the long run."

"Canada?" I asked, unsure of what to think.

"Sure, lots of great players play in Canada.

You'll have a blast, Matt."

"Canada," I said, more assuredly. "Yeah, I guess that'll work." I wasn't thrilled about changing my NFL plans. But I trusted Al. So I was forced to put the Grizzlies on the back burner for now. Besides, practice was starting in a couple of days. If I didn't win that starting quarterback job, my football career would be over anyway.

Less than forty eight hours later, I was sitting on a stool in the locker room. I put on shoulder pads for the first time in nearly five years. I moved around like a nervous kid. It took me a minute to get used to wearing my battle armor again. A few of my teammates were staring at me. A few even shook my hand. They knew how long the road was that I had traveled to make it here.

Although I had many supporters on the team, I also had some enemies. Brent Barber and his crew were giving me a pretty bad vibe. This made me self conscious among my teammates. Something had to change. I knew that a great quarterback had to be a confident leader.

There was a lot of excitement surrounding my return to the football field. The entire campus was talking about me. Some guys on the team were excited too. They'd heard about my high school career. I think this was why Brent was so angry. He'd played here for three years. Now, the fans and some of our teammates were ready to replace him. I just hoped I could live up to the great expectations people had of me.

This situation created some bad blood on our team. Before spring practice even started, there was a heated quarterback controversy. The truth was, I had no idea what would happen. I used to be great, but that was a long time ago.

I stepped out onto the field. My mind flooded with memories of past glory days. The sounds and smells of football filled my nose. It was like the first time I stepped onto that grass when I was a kid. I touched the ground with my fingers. I was home again.

I jogged a warm-up lap around the track and felt like I could run all day. I quickly realized that I was in the best shape of my life. I'd also grown an inch or two. I was now 6'5" with my weight approaching 235 pounds. Bring it on!

Coach Copeland and his six assistants were very demanding. Spring ball was the time to learn the plays and get the timing down. The area that I was sure would present me with the most problems was timing. I had never thrown to these receivers. And I'd never tried to throw a pass with college athletes chasing me either.

The first few days of practice went pretty well. I was jelling with most of my teammates. I felt like I was making progress too. There were no miracles, though. I didn't step onto the field after four years and play like a superstar. I had moments where I looked great and moments where I looked terrible. Everyone was big and fast. The adjustment was greater than I imagined.

Monday was the first day we played full contact. There were twelve days of spring practice in total. We played the "red and yellow game" on the last day. I checked the depth chart on my way into the locker room. I was penciled in at third string. This meant that I had moved up one notch. I was getting closer to where I wanted to be.

Things started moving very quickly on the field that day. There were some major differences between high school and college football. In football, offensive linemen form a wall around the quarterback to protect him. The space they create for the quarterback is called 'the pocket.' The pocket was the place where the college game really changed. In high school, I would stay in the pocket for as long as I needed to. In college, the pocket could collapse on you in an instant. I felt uncomfortable there. I knew that if that continued I was not going to have success passing.

When the ball was snapped, everything went crazy. The defensive linemen grunted and growled a few feet away from me. By the time I saw my receiver I would be on my back. I was having a hard time executing even the simplest of plays. After a fumbled snap, a bad pass, and an interception, Coach Copeland blew his whistle.

"Matt," he said. "You're thinking too much!

Get back, get set, and release!"

I looked over at Brent Barber who was snickering at my mistakes. A couple of other guys were rolling their eyes. A few of them even laughed. "This ain't high school," a big lineman said as he helped me off the ground. I was embarrassing myself on the football field. I'd never done that before. I had to convince my teammates that I was someone they could count on. And I had to do it quickly.

Okay, these guys are faster than anything you've seen. This means you have to be faster. Think quick, move fast. Get back, get set, and release. Coach tossed the ball back to me.

In the next series, I turned it up a notch. Coming to the line, I looked around at my teammates. I was through worrying about what these guys thought. I had to let my talent do the talking.

I took the snap and jumped back with four lightning steps, completing a quick out pattern for a fifteen-yard gain. I threw the ball hard. Eddie Thomas caught the pass easily and pointed his finger at me. On the next play, I tossed a laser right through the teeth of the defense. Toby, my roommate and favorite target, made the catch.

"Great pass, Matt. Now you're getting it." Coach yelled.

I shot a glance over at Barber. I was starting to feel some confidence. I completed every single pass I threw for the remainder of practice. I tossed tight spirals with pinpoint accuracy. Even I was impressed.

By Wednesday, I was number two on the depth chart. I was more comfortable around my teammates now as well. I started acting like myself. I was cracking jokes and having fun. Barber was the starting quarterback, but he could sense me right behind him. We still hadn't spoken a word to one another.

The last week of spring practice ended as quickly as it started. We were pretty well set going into the "red and yellow game." The first offense and the second defense would play against the first defense and the second offense. I would quarterback the second offense. Coach told me he would be watching both Brent and me very carefully. This game would decide who would start next season as the number one quarterback.

Game time was scheduled for 7:30. By 6:30, I was throwing a football in the air and catching it. Toby was sitting on the bench next to me. "We win this game together and we'll be starting once the season gets under way."

I reached out and bumped knuckles with Toby, "I'm with you. We've been through too much to get this close and not make it." Toby and I knew exactly what was at stake.

It seemed strange putting a football jersey on with the number eight on it. I'd always worn number fifteen, from youth football through high school. But Barber wore fifteen, too, so I didn't make a big deal about it. There was one cool thing about this. I told Kenny that my number had changed from fifteen to eight. The next day he asked his football coach if he could switch to eight too.

Coming out onto the field for pre-game warm-ups took my breath away. The stadium was filled to capacity. Kenny was in the stands, sitting with Amy and Al. I hadn't seen Al in the two months since his release. I was excited to have dinner with him after the game. This time we'd eat in a restaurant, not the prison cafeteria.

The crowd did the wave, the band played, and the cheerleaders danced. The sounds of the stadium were awesome.

Barber brought the first offense up to the line of scrimmage. I figured they had something special planned. It didn't matter because Rocky Benson, our big 6'6" defensive tackle, sacked Barber. Rocky beat his man around the outside and leveled Brent. On the next play, Barber tossed a screen pass that gained five yards. The crowd got a little bit louder for Barber's third down attempt. It was batted down at the line of scrimmage by "The Mountain," 300-pound John Schulpes. This brought up fourth down. The red team was forced to punt.

I quickly snapped on my chin strap and ran onto the field. On our first play, from our own thirty-five yard line, I was nervous. Still, in the huddle, I faked confidence. "Listen up, fellas! We're all on the second offense because Coach thinks someone can do it better than we can. Let's show him that we belong in that first team lineup." This comment got everyone fired up. These guys had a lot of pride. They'd all been the best players at their high schools. None of them liked the idea of sitting on the bench.

Everyone on the defense was sure Coach would start me off slow. They expected a dive play to our running back. Instead, we faked a run and I hit Toby for fifteen yards over the middle. We came back with the dive on the next play. Our little freshman tailback, Ruben Flores, picked up eight yards. This was exactly what an offense hoped for, second down and short. You could go for the easy first down or you could go for it all.

I got the signal from the sidelines and smiled. Coach Reid had called for the bomb. I looked the defense over slowly as I walked to the line of scrimmage. I called hike and dropped straight back. My big fullback, Gary Garner, saved me from a sack with a smashing block. Toby ran a deep hook pattern that brought the safety up. Terrell Lewis ran deep. He was two steps ahead of his defender. *Could I throw the ball that far?* I reared back and let loose a cannon. The ball must have sailed for fifty yards. The crowd went wild as the pass landed in Terrell's hands. Touchdown! That was just about the best feeling in the world.

The rest of the night was ours. By the third quarter the whole place was chanting "Devon." Our defense hardly gave Barber a chance. And when they did, his passes floated or came up short. I think he was trying to do too much. We went on to win the game 28 to 6. I had earned my place in the starting lineup.

Amy ran out onto the field just like in high school. Al and Kenny were right by her side. My first semester of school was almost over. I had a lot to look forward to…like my first college football season.

CHAPTER SIX

SUMMER CHAOS

School was over for the semester and I was back in Hobbs. It was going to be a whirlwind summer. One of the first things I had to do was contact my parole officer. Ernie Drew was his name. I had spoken to him over the phone a few times. He seemed like a decent guy. He was happy that I was going to college and playing football. I was lucky he was fair because I didn't have time for setbacks. My schedule was precise.

I was only going to be in town for a month. I had to get a job, see old friends, and get married. Plus, Amy and I planned a week at the Grand Canyon for our honeymoon. We were waiting for Ernie's approval on this.

Usually nobody would hire someone for only a month, but Al came through for me. He needed extra help around the shop. But before I could accept his offer I had to ask Ernie.

I had no trouble finding Ernie's office in Hobbs. I walked through the front door and he smiled warmly. Ernie was different than I expected. "So Matt, I hear you're gonna start at quarterback this fall up in Taos, huh? I'm a big fan. I'll be excited to watch you play. Heard you had a heck of a showing in that red and yellow game. Four touchdowns?"

"Actually, it was only three, sir," I responded. "But I hope I can keep it up and have a great year."

"Well, you did your time like a man." He opened up a folder and read through some papers. "Two years parole? That stinks." He closed the folder and became upbeat. "We've got to play by the rules, though." He said matter-of-factly.

I thanked him for empathizing with my long parole. I mentioned several things that I needed to get his approval on. He had no problem with the wedding and the honeymoon. And he gave me permission to travel wherever my teammates traveled during our football season.

"Mr. Drew," I said hesitantly, "there is one other thing. I need a job for the month. My fiancée, Amy, is going to be a lawyer. She says I need your permission to work someplace where other ex-cons work. Is that right?" I liked Ernie, but I hated asking permission to live my life.

"She's absolutely right," he said.

"Well, there's this baseball card shop in town.

The owner there is a good friend and ex-felon, also. Would you approve of me working there?"

He hesitated for a moment. "Sure, that's fine." It appeared that Ernie was going to make being on parole fairly easy. Still, I didn't feel truly free. I would have to wait another year or so for that privilege.

I headed right for the card shop after leaving Ernie's. I was anxious to see Al and tell him the good news. The shop didn't open for another twenty minutes and Al was out front cleaning the windows. He led me through the front door and I could hardly believe my eyes. Al's Place was truly something special. It was a fairly big store with a great location. I made my way inside and I was like a kid in a candy store. There were autographed pictures of all the stars hanging on the walls. There were shelves loaded with autographed footballs, basketballs, and baseballs. Glass cases were filled with every trading card in print. It was a sports fan's dream. I passed by a leather chair that was shaped like a baseball mitt. The walls were decorated with every limited edition ever made. There wasn't a better shop in New Mexico, maybe the country.

"So what do you think?" Al practically screamed he was so excited.

"This is unbelievable," I reached out and gave him a proud hug.

"Can you work here?" he questioned.

"No problem." I was smiling from ear to ear.

Al smiled back at me. "Back together again. Pretty spacious place, huh?" We both laughed, remembering a time when we *lived* in a space one quarter the size of this.

A few minutes later we hugged goodbye. I couldn't stay in one place for long right now. I had about a million things to do. My next stop was Billy Bryant's. Billy was now the hero of Hobbs. He had made All-American two years in a row while at Oklahoma. He was a first-round draft pick of the Grizzlies. Billy was an amazing player.

He saw my old truck drive up his driveway and came running out the front door. He was wearing a T-shirt that read "New Mexico Grizzlies" across the front. He gave me a bear hug and slapped me on the back. He handed me a T-shirt that was identical to his. "You better get used to these colors, dog. You'll be our quarterback soon."

I smiled at Billy, ignoring the fact that I knew I wasn't eligible to play in the NFL for two years. We went into Billy's house. It was like I'd never left. Billy's mom made us a couple of peanut butter and jelly sandwiches. I felt like I was thirteen again. We sat on the front porch, drinking lemonade. We talked and laughed like we didn't have a care in the world. It was just like old times.

"So I read about your red and yellow game in the *Hobbs Press*."

I laughed, "They wrote about that in the paper?"

"Of course they did, dog. People love you around here. Everyone knows you got a raw deal." Billy kept going, "The papers said you can still play. You threw for four touchdown passes in your first game back?"

"Three touchdowns, that was a misprint," I pushed Billy playfully. "You're the one who's got the real game, the NFL game. I'm just trying to get back on my feet."

"They can't keep you down for long. After this season, you'll be the quarterback for the Grizzlies." He was smiling.

I had a troubled look on my face. "Not quite, Billy. The NFL won't let anyone play in the league if they're on parole," I said, trying to smile. "I'm gonna have to try to make it up in the CFL first. Then I'll see if the NFL is interested."

The mood got a little heavier after that. I don't think Billy knew quite what to say. He wanted our dreams to play out the way we planned them. But life wasn't that simple. Not for me, at least. I changed the subject. We talked about Amy and the wedding. Billy was my best man. He seemed excited for my big day. It was just a few weeks away.

When we stopped talking about the wedding the subject of prison came up. Billy was curious about my time in jail. I didn't like talking about prison and usually tried to avoid the subject. It had been a dark time in my life. Still, Billy's questions didn't let up. Finally, I told him some stories that made him happy he never broke the law.

"Prison was not what I expected, Billy. At night, I'd imagine you and me playing ball together. Then I'd wake up to those cold metal bars. I'd spend my days staring at them." I looked off into space.

Billy tried to sound upbeat. "Well, we've got our whole lives ahead of us now."

"Yeah we do." I smiled. And since Billy had asked me about prison, I decided I would ask him something. "So, I know it's rude to ask about money." I laughed, "But did you really sign a twelve-million–dollar deal? Is that right? Did the Hobbs Press add too many zeros to that number?"

"That was no misprint, dog. Twelve million dollars to play football!" Billy jumped to his feet. "And the papers didn't write about my signing bonus. You gotta see this."

I followed Billy down to his garage. In it, a brand-new red Porsche was parked. He tossed me the keys. "You drive."

Driving that car was a lot of fun. I didn't know where to go, so I drove Billy over to Al's shop. I thought they'd get a kick out of one another. We parked out front. It didn't take long for word to get around that Billy Bryant was there. Nobody else in Hobbs drove around town in a Porsche. As I introduced Al to Billy we were invaded by a swarm of kids. They all wanted Billy to sign their new football cards.

Billy signed a bunch of autographs and spent some time chatting with Al. Then we made our way back to his car and drove away. "Wow Billy, you're some kind of impressive guy," I teased my best friend.

"The darling of Hobbs, New Mexico," he laughed. There was an uncomfortable silence. "You know this should be you getting all this Hobbs glory. You were always a better player than me."

Billy turned up the radio. We drove back to his place without saying much more. I was happy for my best friend. He was a hard worker and deserved success. But at the same time *I* had always been number one around here. Seeing kids pass by me to get to Billy at the card shop was strange. It also provided me with more motivation. Not to beat out Billy, but to play alongside him again.

In a month I would be leading a college football team as the starting quarterback. There was nothing more exciting to me. Forget the NFL, contracts, and signing bonuses. I hadn't led a team onto a football field since I was eighteen. I couldn't wait.

Working in the card shop with Al was a blast. Time flew by and business was good. It didn't hurt that Billy came by the shop every day at five. The two of us would head down to the high school and work out. I couldn't believe Billy! The four years at Oklahoma had done amazing things for him. He was quick like a cat. If I ever became a Grizzly, Billy thought we would win a Super Bowl together. Watching him catch passes out on the field, I believed him.

"So what's your plan, anyway?" Billy asked me. "I know Matt Devon has a plan."

"Well, the plan is to play next season at A&E. Then, hopefully, I'll play well enough to get a contract in Canada for a year. If I do well up there, Amy says she'll be able to get me a tryout with the Grizzlies."

"That's great. But what's Amy doing getting you the tryout? You need to get an agent," Billy said. "I could hook you up with my guy. He's the best."

"Amy's my agent," I said smiling.

"What?"

"That's right. Amy's an NFL Certified Advisor. She passed her test last month," I said proudly.

"Amy's your agent! Now that's a twist." he said.

That month flew by. Before I knew it, my wedding day arrived. We were married on July 21. Billy loaned us his Porsche for our trip to the Grand Canyon. So we headed off on our honeymoon in style.

"Hey Billy," I said smiling, "you can use my truck while I'm gone."

"Thanks pal, but I've got my own truck." He pointed to the lot, where a brand-new black pick-up was parked.

I shook my head. "Celebrity does have its advantages doesn't it?"

Billy pointed to his Grizzlies shirt. "You'll find out soon enough, dog."

CHAPTER SEVEN

FOOTBALL SEASON

Walking into the locker room on the first day of fall practice got me pumped. I wanted to slap my gear on right then and there. I made my way over to a chart posted on the door to Coach Copeland's office. My name was penciled in as the number one quarterback. But that wasn't enough to make me feel comfortable. With the talented Barber at number two, my job was never safe.

A few teammates stepped past me and said hello. Having their confidence behind me was very important. I sipped some water from the fountain near my locker. Brent Barber approached me from the opposite side of the room. "Hey Devon," he called out in a stern voice. *Here it comes*, I thought. This guy was going to give me a hard time on the first day of practice.

"What's up?" I said, extending my hand to shake

with his.

He pushed my arm away. "You know that's my job, right?"

"Not according to Coach," I said, walking away. I couldn't get upset, there was too much at stake.

Barber wasn't finished yet. "Don't turn your back on me, convict." He pushed me and I nearly fell to the floor. When Brent called me a convict I got very upset. It took all the self control I had not to react to him. I turned bright red. I was embarrassed, even hurt. "I'm just here to win, Brent. I'm gonna give everything I've got to take this team to a championship. I'll do that with or without your help." I took another step closer to him and stared into his eyes. "And don't ever call me a convict again, Brent." I walked away from him and took a deep breath.

A few guys on the team heard my short speech and clapped their hands together. My new teammates were behind me in this situation. There was no place for name-calling on a team.

"Quit whining, Brent," I heard somebody yell.

"Let's act like a team!" Someone else called out.

When I looked over at Barber, his head was hung in embarrassment. I actually felt bad for him. I was sure that deep down he was a decent guy. I came along and he was on the bench. It was that simple. He was being a jerk because he loved football so much.

How could I blame him for that? He wanted to play too.

Despite the trouble, we began our season on a hot Monday morning. On the way over to the field, Toby snuck up behind me. He slapped me on my helmet. "You ready?" he screamed.

"I *was* ready, until you smashed my head in." I smiled, shifting my helmet. I turned the conversation down a notch. "I feel bad about Barber. This was his job. What if I can't play like I used to?" Doubt crept into my mind.

"Then it will be his job again," Toby laughed, slapping my helmet again.

The locker room emptied and I was left alone. I took off my helmet and tucked it beneath my left arm. With my mouth wide open, I looked around in awe. If only Mom could see me now. I was walking around in my dreams, but I was wide awake.

I strolled over to my stall where all my gear was neatly placed. The space here was about three times as big as my high school locker. There were three practice jerseys, all red with the number eight on them. They were neatly ironed and placed on yellow hangers. I grabbed one of the jerseys and put my head through it. It stretched over my shoulder pads. The rest of my locker was filled with extra pants, pads, a vest, and socks. On the bottom shelf were three pairs of brand-new red cleats with yellow stripes. I'd imagined staring into a locker like this since I was a little kid.

Before practice started, Coach led us all into the men's gym. We took a seat on the bleachers. He moved to the front and spoke with great power behind his voice. "Welcome men!" We all started to scream. Coach continued, "I hope you are as excited about this season as we are. This team has the potential to be the best group of Cats ever!" This comment was followed by another round of applause from the team. Then Coach grew quieter. "You'll notice that I said potential. Potential is all we have when the season starts. Potential plus hard work makes champions. Without the work, we might as well go home right now. You guys want to go home?" Everyone booed. "Then I guess you're ready to work!" We all stood up and shouted.

I was getting more and more fired up every time Coach opened his mouth. "I saw some nonsense in the locker room a few minutes ago. That is the kind of thing that can break us. It's up to every one of us to be a good teammate. It starts right here and now." Coach paused dramatically and then shouted, "We will be a team!" And with that, Coach stepped down from the podium.

The gym erupted in a loud roar that shook the building. A few seconds later, Brent Barber came up to me. He looked right into my eyes. "I believe in this team, and this team believes in you." Brent and I shook hands. "I won't quit, Matt. I'm going to push you to be better than me every day." I had goose bumps all over, as did the rest of the team. I liked Brent. I liked his honesty and I liked his heart.

As we were leaving the gym, one of the assistant coaches handed us our schedule. Right away, everyone got together. I have to admit, I didn't know much about any of these teams. My attention was always paid to the large schools. Now don't get me wrong, I knew how many NFL players came out of our league. And I knew the High Desert League schedule was by no means easy.

"Why is Crockett State written in all black?" Toby asked while looking over his schedule.

"Beats me, maybe—" but before I could finish my thought Barber chimed in.

"Those are the guys that beat us in the playoffs the last two years. They've got these three receivers that can break the sound barrier." This was what I wanted to hear from Brent, a scouting report.

"What about the rest of these teams? Are they any good?" I asked.

"They're better than most people think. Crockett State, Southern New Mexico, and Delaware could match up with any team in the country."

"You guys ready?" Coach interrupted us. He knew the answer to that question.

A moment later we made our way onto the field. It was about one hundred degrees when we started. Coach let us know that today was going to be spent on conditioning. There were coaches at each twenty-five yard line. They were marking down who was running and who was giving up. They marked down who finished first and who finished last. Coach fueled our practices with competition. This made us work harder. "You've all got talent. But you make my starting lineup with sweat!"

I soon found out that fall practice was where things got serious. These were the best athletes I'd ever been around. And what was even better was that they wanted it as badly as I did. This was especially true of Brent Barber. Six months ago, during spring practice, I ran dead even with Barber in sprints. All summer I conditioned myself by running long distances with Billy. I was confident that when fall practice started, Barber would be in my rearview. I guess he'd been training, too, because he was beating me all day long. As promised, Barber wasn't giving up his starting spot without a fight.

The one drill that everyone hated the most was leap frog. The drill was simple. Each player started in the end zone lined up behind another player. You were to leap frog over the teammate in front of you until you reached the other end zone. You were not allowed to stand up straight. This was the last drill of the day and, by far, the most tiring. What made it extra tough was that there was no finish line. You leaped until you couldn't leap anymore. The last man standing earned the respect of his teammates and Coach Copeland.

The red desert sun began to set in the west. Coach stood above us as we lined up at the goal line in our crouched positions. "We can't rip open your chests and measure the size of your hearts. Instead, we measure it with leap frogs. Whose got the biggest one of the bunch?" And with that, he blew his whistle for us to start. By the fifty yard line, at least half the team dropped off to the side. "Who's got desire on this football team?" Coach yelled. Brent and I were the only two quarterbacks left.

Once we reached the opposite goal line, only three of us remained. There was Barber, myself, and the freshman wide receiver, Trevor Weeks. Weeks ran track in high school. He was probably in the best shape of anyone on the team. Barber and I had no business in the final three. My legs were burning like I'd never felt before. I couldn't give up, though. The look on Barber's face matched mine. Our competition against one another was fueling us beyond our physical abilities. Each of us refused to be the first to drop out.

Weeks eventually went on to win the competition. Brent and I collapsed over each other in the middle of our third lap. When Coach blew the final whistle, the guys carried the two of us back to the locker room.

During the next month or so, we practiced every day. Unfortunately, I was experiencing some problems. The first was that I was under-throwing my receivers at times. I was moving around too much and throwing off of my back foot. If I did this come game time, I was going to throw floating passes that would end up being interceptions. That would be a quick way to find myself on the bench. The second bad habit I'd developed was holding onto the ball too long. This caused me to get sacked a lot in practice. In practice, the defense would let up when they reached me. I knew that once the season began, blitzing defenders were going to clobber me.

I thought about both of these things on our three-hour bus ride down to Princeton, New Mexico. This was the home of the Central New Mexico Bulldogs, our first opponents. Today was the first step in a new beginning for me in football.

The quarterbacks all sat in the front of the bus, near Coach Copeland and Coach Reid. We made a right turn into Sunburst Stadium and I flipped off my headphones. The coaches gave us some last minute advice. Coach Copeland told me something interesting before the game. He started by telling me how impressed he was with the effort that Barber was putting forth in practice. Coach had promised him the opportunity to play in the second half of the game. It was my first game and this didn't really bother me much. In fact, I felt a little relieved. This was a good way to ease me into my first game.

Early on, nothing went the way I planned. On my first play as a college quarterback, a defensive player charged through the middle of our line. I reacted late and stepped backward as I released a pass over the middle. My pass was way short. Their defensive back easily picked it off. He ran right over me on his way to six points. By the time I got back up, the Bulldogs had put a six on the scoreboard. Their crowd was going crazy.

Getting picked off was something that rarely happened to me during my high school career. With the extra point, the Bulldogs grabbed an early 7 to 0 lead.

On the next series I overthrew two receivers and fumbled a snap. The Bulldogs took over and their next possession was flawless. They made some great plays which led to another score and a 14 to 0 lead. This year's Bulldogs squad was the best they'd fielded in a long time. I looked over at the sidelines and noticed Coach Copeland biting his fingernails. He was screaming at everyone too. I also noticed that Brent Barber was warming up. The good news was that Coach hadn't pulled me from the game yet. He was giving me one more drive to set things straight. If I didn't step up, I was going to find myself on the bench.

We started our third possession on our own twenty-yard line after a touchback. Down 14 to 0 on the road, we desperately needed to score. *What if I lost my starting job in the first game of the season? Would I ever get it back?* I shook my head. *Relax, Matt.*

On the first play, the Bulldogs' defense brought everyone in on the blitz. The pocket collapsed before it even formed. Just before I was crushed by two line-backers, I released a screen pass to Sam Golden. This was my first completed pass as a college quarterback. Sam eluded two tacklers and made his way up to the forty yard line. That was a big play. Now I had some breathing room. I gave the ball to Sam again on the next play and he moved us to midfield for another first down. Our offense was developing a rhythm. On the next play, I hit Terrell Lewis on a slant. He made his way to the Bulldogs' thirty-five for another first down. That was my sharpest pass of the game.

Trying to build some momentum, I quickly took the snap. But I failed to see a safety coming from the corner on the blitz. He sacked me easily for a big loss. On second down and eighteen, Toby dropped an easy pass over the middle. Just like that, we were in a bad situation: third down and long.

I'd thrown a few completions, but Barber was still warming up on the sidelines. I took a deep breath and hiked the ball. The defensive pressure came at me immediately. Coach Copeland had been teaching me to step up when I felt the rush. This way my linemen would be able to push the blitz away from me. I'd practiced this for a few months now, but had never tried it in a game. Just before a rushing lineman hit me, I stepped up and fired a laser. The ball sailed into the corner of the end zone. Terrell Lewis was covered closely by a defensive back. The pass cut through the air just over the defender's reach. Terrell pulled it in and spiked the ball in the end zone. I had thrown my first college touchdown pass!

That gave me all the confidence I needed. Barber took a seat on the sidelines. Everything clicked after that. We scored three more times before the half. In a strange half, I'd thrown for three touchdown passes and over 250 yards.

When Brent came in we were pounding the Bulldogs 35 to 14. He was in good form, moving the ball consistently. We scored twice in the second half and won by a final score of 49 to 21. Coach Copeland let the other quarterbacks finish the last five minutes of the game. He'd seen enough. On the bus ride home I was officially named the starter. Coach sat me down in the front seat next to him. "We sink or swim on your shoulders, Matt. This is your team now." This was Coach's quote and was exactly what I wanted to hear.

Next week's road trip was long. We had to cross the border to Amarillo, Texas, for a game against John Hanks College. The coaches said they never knew what to expect when we played Hanks. One year they were good and the next they were terrible. We didn't know which team we'd be facing.

There were about three thousand fans packed into tiny John Hanks Stadium. They were hoping for an upset. But it was not to be. I came out throwing the ball accurately. We moved down the field on six straight passing plays. The final play was a fourteen-yard slant to Henry Dormer for the touchdown. I was feeling comfortable with our offense now.

John Hanks was better than Central New Mexico, but they couldn't keep up with us. By halftime, we had a 28 to 6 lead. This time, Coach Copeland didn't put Barber into the game. I stayed in for a conservative second half. We ran the football on nearly every play. The final score was 41 to 13.

It was a good feeling to win. Still, I couldn't help looking toward next week. The Crockett State Volunteers were coming to town. They'd won their first two games by bigger scores than we had. Against better teams, too.

Practice didn't go right that week. Nothing seemed to break the spell the Volunteers had cast on us. Nobody could forget the last two seasons when we lost to Crockett State. We stumbled through drills. We looked tired as we headed into this game without our confidence.

Our stadium was packed with screaming fans for our first home game. Everyone was fired up for this rematch. But on the opening kickoff, things started off badly. Crockett State's Abner Gentry ran the kickoff back ninety-two yards for a touchdown. That was not the way we wanted to start.

Now it was their turn to kick off to us. Ruben Flores, our kickoff return man, got the ball back to the twenty-five yard line before getting smashed by Donnie Jackson. It's strange how a big hit in a football game can send a strong message to an opponent. After seeing Ruben limp off the field, our body language changed. We looked nervous, checking out the defense. I clapped my hands, signaling that the time had come to get focused.

When I came to the line of scrimmage, I had to calm myself. *Take your time, Matt, don't hurry.* Coach Copeland mentioned that they liked to blitz their safeties. I was sure that one was going to come for me once the ball was hiked. This meant that someone would be uncovered on the left side of the field.

My instincts were right on. I called "hike" and the blitz came at full force. I was able to throw a quick out to the left side that was good for the first down. The problem was that when I released the ball, their cornerback laid his helmet into my chest. He slammed me hard into the ground with the weight of his body. I thought he might have broken one of my ribs because the pain was so bad. I tried to get up, but my chest felt like it would explode. Toby motioned over to the sidelines. The trainer ran out to get me.

Barber warmed up quickly and entered the game. Chip Fickle, our trainer, brought me back into the locker room for x-rays. Meanwhile, back on the field, Barber tried to throw another out pattern to the left side. His pass lacked some zip and a quick cornerback stepped in front of Terrell Lewis. He picked off Barber's effort and headed toward the end zone. Brent tried to make the tackle but wasn't fast enough. The

Volunteers had their second touchdown of the quarter. After just a few plays we trailed 14 to 0.

Back in the locker room, Chip was working as fast as he could. He wrapped my chest in ice and put me under the x-ray machine. He quickly realized that I had not suffered a break. I heard this news and jumped to my feet. "Wait a minute, Matt." Chip wasn't going to let me out there yet. "You need to rest this. If you get hit again, you *will* break it. Then we'll lose you for three weeks instead of just one." Chip had a point.

So I sat in the locker room and iced my ribs for the rest of the first half. By the time the guys came in at halftime, Crockett State had scored ten more points. We were losing 24 to 0.

I told Coach that I was ready to play.

"What about the ribs?" He looked over at Chip, who shrugged his shoulders.

"I can play, Coach. I've been through worse." There was no way he was going to keep me out.

"Okay son." Coach patted me on the shoulder. "Don't try and get it all back at once." I knew Coach was right. We had to take our time. If I forced the issue, the gap would grow.

Things started going our way immediately in the second half. Their return man fumbled the ball on the kickoff and Toby fell on it at the fifteen-yard line. I put my helmet on and stepped onto the field. I moved my arm around in circles to make sure my ribs would hold up. Our crowd went wild. The excitement was in the air. I wanted to go for the touchdown on the first play. Then I remembered what Coach Copeland had said. Instead, we ran an off-tackle play to Sam that got us seven yards.

We were inside their ten-yard line. Now was the time to strike. I hiked the ball and pump faked toward the left side. The blitz came quickly, but I ducked under a linebacker. He dove at the chance to hit my bruised chest. Once he was past me I threw a quick slant to Henry Dormer over the middle of the field. He caught the ball at the two and dove in for the score. The two-point conversion put us back in the game, down 24 to 8.

Crockett State got the ball back and we didn't see it for eight minutes. They ran the ball again and again. We finally stopped them on *our* twenty. They had to settle for a field goal and a 27 to 8 lead.

Offensively, I was on a roll now. Four passes later we'd scored again. This time the touchdown was on a twenty-yard curl to Toby. We got the two point conversion on a quarterback keeper up the middle. The score was now 27 to 16 and I couldn't feel the pain in my chest anymore. At the end of the third, we had a chance.

Again, the Volunteers played clock control. This time they held the ball for almost six minutes but were forced to punt. Their punter got off a beauty that went out-of-bounds at the three. Seven minutes remained and we needed to score twice. Ninety-seven yards was a long way to travel. It would be tough, but not impossible.

The first play went for twenty yards as Toby reached out and made a great catch. He was finally dragged down on the twenty-four yard line. We ran the ball to Sam on the following play. Our offense was quickly coming to the line now. I passed to Toby again. Then I threw to Terrell Lewis downfield. I even ran a few times when nobody was open. Before we knew it, we were knocking on the door again.

From the Volunteers thirty-six yard line, I threw a lofting pass over the defense that dropped into the arms of Buddy Johnson. He caught the ball in stride and fell into the end zone. Touchdown! Another successful two-point conversion and we were down 27 to 24. There were three minutes and ten seconds left to play

We could feel it! Everyone in the stands was on their feet.

We kicked the ball into the hands of the Volunteers' wide receiver, Napoleon Kennedy. And then something terrible happened. Napoleon marched right through us for a ninety-yard touchdown run. I had never been more upset on a football field.

We'd tried, but came up short. I walked off the field that day with aching ribs and a broken heart. It was the first loss I had ever suffered on a football field. All I could hope for was that we'd get another shot at Crockett State in the playoffs.

CHAPTER EIGHT

WINNING SEASON

My ribs grew less and less sore with each passing day. Still, I felt anxious during the following week of practice. That loss really played tricks on my brain. Each time my legs tired or my arm began to ache, I thought about losing. This wasn't helping me play well.

When Southern New Mexico rolled into town, my fear of losing was still fresh. I started that game in a panic. I was playing football like it was a matter of life and death. Fear had taken over. I began forcing passes to my receivers and rushing my delivery.

Late in the first quarter, though, something changed. I was looking into the stands to catch a glimpse of Amy. Instead, I noticed a young boy. He was wearing a youth football jersey. He reminded me of a younger version of myself. I was brought back to the football days of my youth. With great memories in my mind, I brought the team to the line of scrimmage.

My goal was simple—have fun and play to win.

I became excited as I received the snap from center. My confidence was building. When the pocket collapsed and the linemen came at me I was calm. Instead of throwing a bad pass, I rolled out to my right. This was something I rarely had done in my short college career. I was playing on instincts again, not worrying about failure. Rolling out was the right decision. I'd shed the defense. When I looked up, the entire field was in front of me. Toby was running a deep tight end drag and he was open. I set my feet and chucked a spiral thirty yards through the desert air. My giant friend caught it at midfield and rambled in for a touchdown. That was the beginning of a great day for us.

For the rest of that afternoon, I played great. I ended up hitting on twenty of twenty-seven passes for 353 yards and two more touchdowns. Coming into that game, all we heard about was the Southern New Mexico defense. Instead of fearing them, we lit them up 31 to 10.

That win helped me to become my old self again. I was glad, because our next game would probably be our biggest test of the season. We were confident and self-assured as we made our longest road trip of the year. We flew halfway across the country to meet with the third ranked Delaware State Saints. They were a team known for their size and strength.

Coach Copeland told us that the Saints would

be the biggest team we'd play all year long. All five of their offensive linemen weighed close to 300 pounds. This made getting pressure on their quarterback tough. Our biggest advantage over Delaware State was speed. Besides their quick quarterback, Mercury Brooks, we were faster at nearly every position. Coach came up with a game plan that used our speed to wear down our opponents.

Playing on the east coast during the winter was always an adventure. The weather was certainly a factor in this one. An icy wind blew across the field in strong gusts. On our first offensive play, I took a three-step drop and hit Terrell Lewis. The wind was really affecting my passes. Coach reminded me to keep the ball low. Anything that hung up there in that wind was dangerous. Over the next four minutes we owned Delaware's excellent defense. With quick drops and short passes, we had them on their heels. We moved right down the field.

On first and goal from the nine, the crowd was on their feet. I noticed both of their inside linebackers had moved outside of our tackles. I called "hike" and took a five-step drop. As the pocket collapsed, I made a dash for the goal line. It worked like a charm. I went into the end zone standing up for our first touchdown. We kicked the extra point to go up 7 to 0.

The rest of that game was uneventful. Their defense tightened and the wind picked up, making it difficult to move the football. We didn't score our second touchdown until late in the fourth quarter on a long run by Sam Golden. With only two minutes left and a 14 to 0 lead, we knew we'd won the game. We'd beaten one of the best teams we'd face all year long. The credit for that win went to our defense.

Everything went our way for the rest of the regular season. We were scoring about forty points a game and allowing only about thirteen. We finished the year with a record of 10 and 1 and earned the number two seed in the championship tournament.

In our final regular season game, we pounded Canton in front of our home fans. After the game, Coach Copeland got us all together in the locker room. "This team will not be measured by a ten and one season. We'll only be remembered when we win the whole thing. The playoffs start next week, men!" We all cheered loudly. "It looks like we play Northern California. So go home and enjoy tonight, but be ready to work tomorrow. Starting Monday, the second season begins."

We'd be facing Northern California in the first round of the playoffs. They were the biggest loudmouths in the league. Hopefully for us, their bark was stronger than their bite.

Amy and Al had come up for the game and we went to dinner afterwards. We picked up Kenny on the way to the restaurant. We all ate steaks and talked about old times. Kenny told us stories about leading his football team to the championship game. I listened with a huge smile on my face. It was the best dinner I'd ever had. I remembered a time when I felt like I was alone in the world. My eyes met Kenny's during dessert. I knew that no matter what happened with my football career, I was a lucky person.

When I woke up Sunday morning, the city of Taos was buzzing. The entire state of New Mexico was fired up about our chance at a championship. I was even on a radio talk show.

Coach tried to make it extra clear that we needed to stay focused on the first game. If we looked past next week we'd get beat. I couldn't afford to miss the opportunity to play on television. I knew that only our second-round games would be aired. A win would get me a ticket to the second round and national television exposure.

There had been a few pro scouts at our games throughout the season. I knew there'd be quite a few more come playoff time. Undoubtedly, they would be there to scout some of our big linemen. But something unexpected happened to me four days before our game. A scout from the Edmonton Eskimos had been down all week to watch practice. I figured he was looking at John Schulpes, who was being heavily recruited. Instead, the scout informed me that he'd come down from Canada to see me play. Sam Hanson was his name. He was the head scout for the Eskimos. He told me that the Eskimos veteran quarterback had recently retired. If I were to get drafted, I'd be competing with a few other guys for his job.

So far, I hadn't received any attention from pro scouts in any league. I think teams were assuming that I was a 'problem player' because of my criminal record. Not one of them took the time to get to know me. I was beginning to see how much of an effect my time in prison had on my name.

Three days before the big playoff game, Amy and I were having dinner in our apartment. "I bet you can't guess where I'm going tomorrow." She spoke as she took a bite of her mashed potatoes.

"I didn't know you were going anywhere," I said. Amy was smiling from ear to ear. "Where are you going?" I asked.

"I'm going to Edmonton!" she exclaimed.

"Edmonton? Why?" I took a large sip of water.

"I'm going to represent the best college football player in the country," she exclaimed. She came around the table and sat on my lap.

I nearly spit my water out when she said that. "What do you mean, Amy? I can't sign a contract yet. I can't even have an agent." The look on my face was both concerned and excited.

"Well, you're right on the first piece of business. You can't sign a contract until you're done playing college ball. But we can have everything agreed upon in advance. As far as having an agent, you're in good shape. I can represent you legally because you're my husband."

I was smiling now. "So you're going to Canada?"

"Yup, and Al's going with me. The Eskimos are paying for all our expenses."

"But Mr. Hanson said that he wanted to see me play in that playoff game and—"

Amy cut me off. "He's seen enough. He wants to make you an offer before anyone else does."

"This is unbelievable!" I stood up and lifted Amy as high as I could. I put her down a moment later as the usual doubts began to creep into my head. "Do they know about—" I paused. "Do they know my history? I mean, do they know what I did?"

"Yes, they know everything. They want you to be their quarterback, Matt. They know you're a great person, too." Amy kissed my head. "Sam Hanson told me that he'd sign you today if he could."

Amy and Al left for Canada around noon. They would arrive back in New Mexico just after eight. Although I tried not to, I did think about them a few times that day. Still, I was very focused during practice. I felt ready to take on any team in the country.

Twenty minutes after practice ended, I was at the airport. Their plane came in ten minutes early and they were the first off. "So?" I asked them. Nobody spoke a word. Their faces were blank. They looked tired and disappointed. My heart sunk to my stomach. Something had gone wrong. I grabbed their luggage and walked toward the parking lot silently. It appeared as if my dreams had been put on hold again.

We made it to the car and I looked over at Amy. "So what happened? I thought this was gonna be easy."

"Well," her frown quickly turned into a smile.

"It *was* easy. My husband will be a well-paid professional quarterback for the Eskimos next season!" Al let out a big laugh from the back seat. He and Amy had been waiting to pull that trick on me.

"Are you serious?" I screamed.

"Yup." Amy answered.

I banged my hands on the roof and screamed again. "You did it! They went for your offer."

Al chimed in. "Even better. By the time she was through with them, their offer was twice what we'd hoped for."

Amy looked like an angel sitting next to me. I felt as if I owed all of this to her. In my jail cell at night, playing professional football had been a distant dream. Now that dream was real.

CHAPTER NINE

THE PLAYOFFS

Finally, the playoffs arrived. Coach Copeland gave us a short speech in the locker room. Everyone stood on one knee in front of him. "Let's deliver a message right off the bat to these loudmouths. And let's deliver our message with big plays and great tackles. Nobody on this team talks trash. Winning the football game is all the talking you need to do today. See it and execute it."

See it and execute it. See it and execute it. Those words echoed in my head as I waited at the top of Cat Hill. There was a tradition that we had for playoff home games. The entire team would stand on top of Cat Hill. This was the hill behind the scoreboard. We'd come running down in our red uniforms screaming like lunatics.

We were off and running. Like eighty bolts of lightning, we took the field. From the stands, we sounded like a herd of buffalo. After that, Northern California began their talking. We could hear them from across the field during warm-ups. None of us responded and I think our silence shook them up.

When the game started, we began with the ball on the twenty. On first down we ran a quick draw play left. It took their defense completely by surprise. They were sure we'd come out throwing. They had called a blitz so their defense was charging in. I handed the ball to our fullback. Sam smashed through the middle of their line. He took off into the open field with the defense chasing him down. He ran forty-two yards before being brought down from behind. Northern California's trash talking slowed after that.

The ball was on our opponent's thirty-five. I threw my first pass of the playoffs to Toby. He made a great one-handed catch. "Good grab," I slapped his helmet in the huddle.

I called "hike" on the next play, hitting Terrell Lewis for a fifteen-yard deep curl. On the next play, I hit Toby again for ten yards. I was entering the zone and seeing the field clearly. Their defense sensed this and dropped back into coverage. This opened things up for our running game. With the defense confused, we went back up the middle to Sam Golden. He ran into the end zone untouched. We went ahead 7 to 0 on our opening drive.

The rest of the day was much of the same. I threw for 223 yards and three touchdown passes in the first half! Barber came in for the second half and threw three more. The final score was a brutal 51 to 6.

After the game, Coach Copeland congratulated us on a great win. He also let us know that Delaware and Crockett State had won big today. Next week, we'd face Delaware. And that didn't excite us much.

The next day we arrived in Kansas. Coach wanted us to get the feel for the Kansas weather so he had us practice in shorts. We felt it all right. The temperature was twenty-three degrees with snow flurries. The snow was supposed to be even heavier for our game on Saturday. This was bad news for us. We were the better offensive team, but bad weather usually creates a defensive game. This would play to Delaware's advantage.

Despite the forecast, we were ready to play the game. On Saturday we boarded the bus to Flatland Stadium. Looking out my window, I was impressed to see tons football fans packed into the parking lot.

Twenty minutes later I was in full uniform. The game couldn't start quick enough for me. Coach Copeland walked into the locker room covered in heaps of snow. "It's coming down out there, boys." This was troubling news. We'd talked a great deal about the weather during our offensive meetings. If the snow didn't allow us to pass the ball, we'd rely on our running backs.

When we got outside I couldn't believe my eyes. The snow was falling hard and fast. I could barely see in front of me. We won the toss and elected to kick-off. Their first possession went nowhere. Their talented quarterback, Mercury Brooks, tossed his lone pass attempt into the stands. It was clear that the passing game was going to be slowed by the snow. Three quick offensive plays led to a Saints punt.

We got the ball on our own thirty-six yard line. On first down we ran a draw play that gained fifteen yards. That was a huge play for a first down run. We'd definitely caught them off guard. So with the ball at the fifty, we tried to keep them off balance. A fake dive up the gut on the following play confused everyone. I pulled back and hit Toby on a quick slant. He broke a tackle and was off and running. He rumbled toward the end zone with only one man to beat. Darrel Foster, the speedy safety, ran toward him from the sideline. Toby never saw him coming. Foster chopped at Toby's arm with the power of his legs behind him. The ball popped loose just before Toby crossed the goal line. Another Saints defender slid in and grabbed the leather on the six. That turnover was enormous.

Things got worse on the next play. Mercury Brooks dropped back into the pocket and looked as if he were going to throw. With our defense closing in quickly he pumped deep downfield. Everyone left their feet. Everyone but Mercury. He pulled the ball down and took off. He was the fastest quarterback we'd faced all season. Tackling him was difficult. But tackling him on the slippery snow was nearly impossible.

One lineman after another slid, flopped, and missed Mercury. Before we knew what happened, he was sprinting down the sidelines. There was nothing in front of him but the end zone. He ran it in ninety four yards from his own six yard line! We found ourselves trailing 7 to 0. Toby's fumble was a fourteen-point swing.

My face felt like it was frozen solid on the next possession. The guys huddled around me. Everyone looked upset after falling behind so quickly. I needed to lighten our spirits. "Heck of a run by Mercury, huh? You guys think these legs could scamper for ninety-four?"

Terrell Lewis answered me, "My baby sister could outrun you, Matt." Everyone laughed. I could feel them loosen up a bit.

"Let's even the score." Being a quarterback wasn't all about passing and running. It was also about being a confident leader.

I walked up to the line of scrimmage and licked my right hand. This was a sure indicator that I was going to throw the football. This small movement dropped the Saints' linebackers back. Instead of throwing, I handed the ball to Sam. He ran up the middle for six yards. We ran the same play twice more and earned a first down.

I looked to the sidelines for the signal. *Great call,* I thought to myself. We were going with a play action pass. This meant that after the ball was snapped, I would fake the handoff. When the defense came in,

I would drop back and throw.

After running three times in a row, everyone fell for my fake. I stepped back in the pocket and everyone was open. I threw a tight spiral through the wind downfield. It landed right in Terrell Lewis's arms—and fell through them. I clapped my hands in frustration. That one should've been a touchdown.

Much of the first half went that way. We managed to put a field goal on the board, but so did the Saints. Despite the fact that we had dominated the game, we trailed 10 to 3 at halftime.

We got the ball to open the second half and moved down the field. Still, we were stopped on third down on the twenty-five. Sam slipped on an ice patch in the backfield and lost a yard. That brought up fourth down and another field goal attempt. The temperature was dropping and we were trailing 10 to 6.

When Delaware got the ball back they were determined. Their running game was powerful. They pounded our defense up the field as the clock ticked down. They seemed to be unstoppable. Before we knew what happened, the third quarter was coming to a close.

On the first play of the fourth, Delaware landed a knockout punch. On third down and four from our thirty-yard line, Mercury faked a handoff left. Our entire defense bit, running left. But Mercury rolled right and there was nobody in front of him. He strolled thirty yards into the end zone without being touched.

The extra point split the uprights and the score was 17 to 6, Saints.

We tried to mount a comeback, but it was no use. The snow was so heavy that our offense just wasn't working. Like many things in my life, there was no storybook ending. We didn't win my last college football game. We didn't move on to face Crockett State. And we didn't capture the national championship. Maybe it was the snow or the turnovers. Either way, we'd lost.

The good news was that the Eskimos called Amy after the game. They had a copy of my contract ready for me to sign.

The flight home was pretty smooth, but my mind was in knots. Once we were in the air for a few minutes, Toby walked over. He sat next to Amy. He had a strange look on his face, like he was uncomfortable. "I need to ask you something."

"Sure, what's up?" asked a confused Amy.

"Well, last week, a couple of scouts from the Grizzlies came up to me. They said they were interested in me. They asked me if I had an agent," said Toby. "I told them no."

"Good answer. So what do you want to do?" Amy asked, taking out a pen and paper and jotting down some notes.

"Well, I want to play pro ball, but I didn't think things would happen so quickly. I'm not getting any younger. I was thinking that I could try to play in the

NFL next year."

"I think you could play for the Grizzlies right now." Amy was using her lawyer voice now.

"Really? What do you think Matt?" Toby was looking at me.

"You're better than half the tight ends in the league. Plus, you're as big as a truck. You can't teach size, that's what Coach Copeland says."

"Okay, so what do I do now, Mrs. Agent?" Toby asked Amy. "How do I sign you up?"

"Sign me up?" Amy asked.

"Yeah," Toby was smiling.

"Are you asking me to be your agent?" Amy was a little startled.

"Yeah. If you can get this guy signed, imagine what you could do for me." Toby laughed.

"Okay, come by my office tomorrow." She extended her tiny hand and shook it with his massive one.

Amy looked at me. "That was something I didn't expect."

"I'll be married to the biggest sports agent in the business." I kissed her proudly, trying to be happy despite our loss.

I signed my contract with Edmonton when our plane landed in Taos. It was official. I was a professional football player. Things were coming together. I finished the semester at A&E and Amy set up her office in Edmonton.

CHAPTER TEN

PRO FOOTBALL

When Billy and I spoke, it was obvious that he was frustrated. The Grizzlies quarterback just wasn't clicking with him. Billy wanted *me* throwing the ball to him. He would end our conversations the same way every time. "I can't wait until you're throwing me touchdowns, dog." That sounded exciting. But for now, I was focused on beginning my career with the Eskimos.

April arrived before we knew it. That meant the NFL draft. This was a great day for Amy and Toby, but a difficult day for me. *Why had I done such a stupid thing when I was a kid?* It had already cost me four years of my life. Now it was costing me a chance to be drafted in the NFL.

The contract Amy got for Toby made her a lot of money. I couldn't have been happier for them both. The Grizzlies thought that Toby could be a starter within a year. It was easy to make him a young millionaire. Amy's three percent came out to about $100,000. It was the most money we had ever seen.

Amy got herself some clothes and we got a new car, too. The only other thing that I bought was a round-trip plane ticket for Kenny. He came up to Edmonton after school let out. Kenny was going to stay with us for the month of June. This was the first month of the football season.

As for football, I was going to have the opportunity to compete for the starting job. For me, this was more exciting than money. If I'd been drafted by an NFL team I would spend at least one season on the bench. Being in Canada during my rookie season couldn't have worked out better.

I left for Edmonton on May 15 to start my career. I drove Amy's new black Corvette all the way up north. I was glad that I got to Edmonton early. I quickly got a feel for the team and the city as well. The population was 720,000, but it seemed even bigger. Commonwealth Stadium, the place I would call home on the football field, was awesome. That grass field was like nothing I had ever seen.

The first day of practice was exciting for me. Someone was actually going to pay me to throw a football! I couldn't get over this. Yes, I'd had some tough breaks in my life. Yes, things had been rough at times. I tossed a deep pass to a wide receiver. *But how could I have ever gotten so down about my life?*

I wondered.

Head Coach John Clarke approached and spoke his first words to me. "I hear you're the most exciting thing we've got around here."

"Thank you, sir," I smiled.

"Exciting is good. Winning's better." He looked right into my eyes. "Can you win?"

"Yes sir."

"Good," Coach patted me on the back and walked away.

The hardest thing for me was adjusting to football in Canada. There were all these rule changes, and the field was different too. The field was 110 yards long and 65 yards wide. This was longer and wider than an NFL field. There were three plays per possession instead of four. This meant that passing was a bigger part of the game. You had twelve players on the field instead of eleven, too. This gave you a better chance of getting a first down on just two or three plays.

Another major difference was that in Canada we played two games a week. In America they only played one. Plus, our calendar was different. We started in June and ended with the Grey Cup, Canada's Super Bowl, in November. Despite all these differences, it was football any way you sliced it. It took some time, but I got used to things up north.

I was challenging two other rookies and one free agent for the starting job. The free agent was probably my biggest rival. Bimbo Johnson had been out-standing in college, but he had limited success in the NFL. He was a backup one year with Green Bay and played a little with San Diego. Cocky was the best word to describe Bimbo. The best rookie I was competing with was Steve Spencer. He was last year's quarterback at Auburn.

In the NFL all the receivers had to stand still until the ball was snapped. But in Canada receivers could wind up and get a ten-yard running start. This changed my timing, but I got used to it. I often wondered how anyone would be able to cover Billy Bryant with these rules. Overall, the Canadian game was more offensive than the American game. This didn't bother me at all.

To my delight, I was named the starter for our first preseason game. Hamilton, the team we were facing, got the ball first. I was glad. This gave me a chance to see things up close. On the opening drive they put together two first downs and had to punt.

Coach grabbed me by the arm on my way onto the field. "You call the first play. Then the show's mine," he said smiling.

In the huddle everyone was waiting to see what play I would call. By the look in their eyes, I could see that they didn't have confidence in me yet. That was fine by me. I'd have to prove myself to them first. I was sure that eventually they'd all believe in me.

I looked over at Daryl Jennings, my closest

friend on the team so far. "D," I said, "How about running a ten-yard slant?"

Daryl nodded his head.

I came up to the line of scrimmage and started calling signals. I didn't pay any attention to the defense or the crowd. I wanted to keep my first play simple. All my energy was focused on Daryl and the quick slant. I called "hike" and the blitz came at me fast. Right away I hit Daryl. He caught my pass in stride and broke free from coverage. He had some room to run down the sideline. In fact, he had all the room he needed. I couldn't believe it, but my first play as a professional was a seventy-four yard touch-down!

Coach was laughing when I came over to the sidelines. "Can you do that again? If you can, I'm out of the job."

I played the first half, throwing for 180 yards and two touchdowns, both to Daryl. By the end of that half I was beginning to see that look in my team-mates' eyes. I was quickly winning them over. Bimbo Johnson came in for the second half. He tossed three interceptions and screamed at our receivers the entire time. We still ended up winning 30 to 24. But Bimbo assured himself a spot on the bench. Steve Spencer would play the second half of our next game. If I played well again, I was sure the starting job would be mine.

The rest of the preseason went pretty much the

same way. Spencer played the next week and was okay. But he wasn't good enough to steal the spot from me. Coach Clarke announced in a press conference that I would be the starting quarterback. This was surprising to some of the media. They thought that since I had no experience, Coach would give me a year to learn.

Our final game of the preseason was against Ottawa. Coach let me play all four quarters. We humiliated them on their home field, 43 to 7. I had thrown for 362 yards and a touchdown. Suddenly, the Canadian media was in love with me. They made big predictions about our season. They talked about my experience in prison and all it had taught me. They even wrote an article about Amy being my agent.

I couldn't believe the way the Edmonton fans responded! There were a few thousand people greeting us at the airport after our final preseason game. Everywhere we went I was swamped for autographs. It was more fun than I had imagined.

A week later, with the people of Edmonton glued to their television sets, we began our regular season against Winnipeg. The game was exciting, with the lead changing hands just about every time the ball did. Our offense was on, but so was theirs. We knew that whoever had the ball last would have the best chance to win. With two minutes left, we were that team.

We were eighty yards away from a touchdown, and the score was 38 to 34 in their favor. A field goal wouldn't do us any good. We needed to drive the length of the field. *Matt Devon, the rookie quarterback was running the two-minute drill in his first professional game.* This was the stuff dreams were made of.

The crowd stood on their feet as they awaited our final drive. I started out with short passes to our running backs. Then I hit our tight end twice. We were moving up the field quickly. With ninety seconds remaining, I took the ball myself and scrambled out-of-bounds. This stopped the clock at midfield. We had no timeouts left. I threw two more completions as the clock continued to tick. I was picking apart Winnepeg's defense like a surgeon. Another completion, and then another. I was seven for eight on this drive so far.

I came to the huddle and called the next play. All eyes were focused on me. Everyone knew what was coming. I didn't disappoint them. With eleven seconds remaining, I hit Todd Wilson in the corner of the end zone. Touchdown! I pumped my fist and was lifted into the air by two of my linemen. One game— one last second victory! I couldn't imagine a greater feeling.

It was extra special because Kenny was there. Afterwards he told me that I was slow. He said that I held onto the ball too long. Other than that he said I'd played great. I laughed, wondering what my nephew would have said if we'd lost. Al came up for that game too and Amy got the three of them seats on the fifty-yard line.

Three days later, we won our second game. I threw three more touchdown passes and was named CFL Player of the Week. The crowd was even bigger at the Edmonton airport this time. Everyone was excited. The following week we would be playing our first home game. And we'd be playing against the defending Grey Cup champs. The British Columbia Lions were always the flashiest team in the league. They were also the team Coach Clarke liked beating most.

The Lions got on the scoreboard first. Joe Burns, their fastest wide receiver, went sixty yards to the house. Despite their early score, there was no doubt about the outcome of this game. We answered their touchdown with four of our own by halftime. Everything we tried worked. Our defense was nasty too. The Lions may have looked flashy, but we won big, 42 to 12.

With three wins and no losses, we were being called the most exciting team in the CFL. We played a wide-open game in the CFL. I usually threw the ball about forty times, sometimes fifty or sixty. This was another reason I loved football up north—I really got to throw the ball.

After three weeks, we were perfect, six wins and no losses. In our seventh game, I ran into an old friend and our streak came to a halt. We played Calgary on a cold Saturday afternoon. At quarterback for the Stampeders was Brent Barber. They'd won two of three games since Brent was named the starter. I was happy for him.

The cold got to me that day and I played poorly. It was an ugly contest. For Brent, that victory was beautiful. Beating the guy who played in front of him in college had to be extra sweet. Calgary pounded us 23 to 7.

We bounced back after that loss and continued our winning ways. By the halfway point of the season, we were 8 and 1. Amy had already started to talk to the Grizzlies about next season. They seemed very interested. *Was I interested in them?* I wondered. I loved Canadian football. The Edmonton fans, my teammates, and the passing game too. It was going to take a lot for me to leave.

The second half of the season arrived. Al flew up to see our big game against Toronto. They were undefeated coming in. We not only beat them 42 to 26, but I played my best game of the season. I threw for over 400 yards and 5 touchdowns!

That was the way the rest of the season went. By the end, it was no surprise that we were the Western Conference Champions. Although we had expected to play Toronto for the championship, Montreal upset them. We'd be facing off for the Grey Cup. What a rookie season! I was going to the Grey Cup in just my first year.

We ended with the best record in the league. This meant that the game would be held in Edmonton.

The week leading up to the big game was hectic. This was Canada's version of the Super Bowl and it had all the same excitement. There were press conferences and reporters everywhere. It was tough to concentrate, but at the same time it was a lot of fun.

With all this stardom, though, came controversy. The questions I was dreading started coming at me often. Reporters continually asked about my mistake and my time in prison. It was hard for me. Sometimes people just made stuff up: "Isn't it true that you were using drugs at the time of your arrest?" "Matt, was your wife in on the robberies with you?" "Are you still on parole?

I answered yes, and everyone went nuts. "You mean your first day as a free man will be the Grey Cup?" Cameras flashed and reporters anxiously jotted down notes.

The press conference ended in a blur. The reporters cleared the room and once again, no one was talking about football. They were talking about my parole. They were talking about my mistake. I woke up the next morning and my parole story was on the cover of every paper in Canada.

The headlines really upset me. All I wanted was to be known as a great person and a great player. But Matt Devon the convict was all people wanted to talk about. I couldn't escape my past.

CHAPTER ELEVEN

THE CUP

At 11:55 on Saturday night, Amy and I stared at the clock. In five minutes I would truly be free. No more parole, no more restrictions. In five minutes, I could start my life fresh. The clock struck midnight. Amy cried. I stared ahead blankly. I didn't know what to think. I put my head on my pillow and fell asleep.

When I arrived at the stadium on Sunday, electricity was in the air. I hopped out of my car and walked through a crowd of 10,000 people. When I stepped out onto the field I couldn't believe my eyes. There were 62,218 crazed fans packed into Commonwealth Stadium. The noise level was unbelievable!

Although the excitement was great, there *was* still a football game to be played. We won the coin toss and decided to receive. The opening kickoff was a shank that bounced toward the sidelines. We started with the ball near midfield.

On first down I brought our guys to the line of scrimmage with a big smile on my face. I walked slowly to the center, licking my fingers. It felt great to be on the field in such an important game. On that first play, the whole stadium knew a pass was coming. Passing on first down had been part of our strategy all year long.

On the first down of the Grey Cup we didn't disappoint. We went for it all. Daryl ran a quick out and then turned on the jets. Nobody could catch him once he got going. I released a long toss. He caught it at the fifteen and ran into the end zone standing up. Just as we had in my first game as an Eskimo, we scored a touchdown on the first play. After that, all of my jitters disappeared. That play set the tone for the first half. Montreal's defense couldn't do anything right. We scored twice more by halftime.

When the third quarter began, we found out quickly that Montreal wasn't through. They came out smoking to start the second half. They took the opening drive right down the field for a touchdown. Their two-point conversion attempt was good as well. This put them back in the game, down 21 to 8.

Chuck Simpson fumbled the ball on the second play of our next possession. Montreal picked it up and ran it all the way in for another touchdown. Again, the two-point conversion was good. Our twenty-one–point lead had shrunk to five. And Montreal was fired up.

But on the next kickoff, Daryl made the biggest run of his life. He took the ball ninety yards for a touchdown. That really let the air out of the Montreal balloon. They never got back into it after that. And I began to heat up. What followed was the best fourth quarter of my career. Leading 28 to 16, I completed thirteen of my next fifteen passes. I threw two more touchdowns to clinch the game. The final score was 42 to 16.

The Edmonton Eskimos were Grey Cup champions!

After the game, the locker room was crazy! We partied for hours with our friends and families. Amy came down with Al and Kenny. It was the celebration I'd always dreamed of. I only wished Mom could have been there too.

After a shower, I was ready to make my way home. When I exited the locker room, reporters swarmed me. They all had questions about my future plans. Some had heard rumors about the Grizzlies. They wanted to know if I'd be playing in the NFL next season. I avoided answering these questions. I told everyone that I wouldn't be making my decision any time soon. I wanted to enjoy this victory.

I left the reporters and felt great. For the first time since I had become a professional, no one asked about prison. They didn't ask questions about my character. They didn't talk about my parole or the big mistake of my youth. I felt free for the first time since high school.

I tried to enjoy the moment on my drive back home. But the only thought in my head was: NFL or the CFL? This was a tough choice. I came to Canada kicking and screaming, but now I was on top of the world.

I grew up in the United States. And sure, I'd always dreamed about playing in the NFL. But then I spent a season up in Edmonton—a magical season. Playing for the Eskimos was the greatest football experience of my life. I couldn't imagine a greater organization or city. *How could I willingly walk away from all of that?* On the other hand, there was the NFL. There was Billy Bryant and the Grizzlies. Playing together had been our dream since we were eight years old. I got goose bumps just thinking about it. That opportunity was finally real. This would mean the chance at being known as one of the greatest. *Was that really what I wanted? Could I pass that up to play for the city of Edmonton?* I didn't have answers to these questions.

The following morning, two faxes came through on our machine. One was from the Grizzlies and one from the Eskimos. They offered me two very similar contracts to play for them the following season.

I didn't answer either of the faxes right away. I just wanted to get back to thinking about football. There was no place better to do that than at a football game. So I flew down to Hobbs to watch another Devon play in a championship game. Kenny's youth football team was playing for the New Mexico State Championship.

I was invited to do the coin toss in the middle of my old high school field. The whole town turned out. Standing at midfield with Kenny was the greatest moment of all. I felt the warmth of hundreds of friendly smiles. These were my people and they were proud of me.

I watched Kenny play an impressive game that day. He was accurate with most of his passes. He even connected on some long ones. And boy could he run! He must have inherited different genes than I did.

But I didn't just watch Kenny play. I watched all the players. I was watching the greatest sport in the world: football. The game is so awesome. You march like an army up the field. The quarterback, the general, commands his team. Everything is on the line on every play. An interception, a fumble, or even a bad snap can sink your ship.

Across the line of scrimmage, the defense waits. They, too, want to make a play and turn the game. But they have to penetrate your line first. That's the beating heart of an offense. If anyone slacks, the machine breaks down. And for the defense, it's the same thing.

The only thing that separates the teams is the twelfth man—confidence. One team gains it and every facial expression on the field changes. You can see right away who has the advantage. That day, I watched Kenny's offense move through the defense near the end of the game. The defense was confused and on their heels. They were reacting to the offense instead of having the offense react to them.

I watched Kenny, today's general. He found a teammate open in the end zone. He fired a pass perfectly into his chest. Eleven pairs of arms raised in triumph. They'd earned a victory together. I saw the smile on Kenny's face and I knew the feeling he was experiencing. Because this game isn't about Super Bowl rings or money. It's about the feeling you get when you've fought your way into that end zone. It's about the looks on the faces of twenty-two players— half in triumph and half in defeat. This is the definition of football.

Coming out to that game I realized that everything would be great—Eskimos or Grizzlies. I knew this because either way, I'd be playing football. And that was what I was born to do.

After earning the 21 to 20 victory, my nephew stood in full uniform next to me. Looking at him holding his MVP trophy in his hands made me proud. It's funny the way life works. If it wasn't for Kenny getting left on our doorstep, who knows where I'd be? I would never have broken the law. Maybe I could have even taken the straight road to the NFL.

Looking down at Kenny, though, I just knew that everything happened for a reason. He was meant to be a big part of my life. I was meant to win the Grey Cup in Canada and to meet Al and play in Edmonton. I'd taken the long way around in my life. Sure, I wish I could have done things differently, but I was definitely on my way to making all my dreams come true.